PERSUASION

USA TODAY BESTSELLING AUTHOR

T.K. LEIGH

BOOKS BY T.K. LEIGH

ROMANTIC SUSPENSE

The Temptation Series

Temptation

Persuasion

Provocation

Obsession

The Broken Crown Trilogy

Royal Creed

Fallen Knight

Broken Crown

For more information on any of these titles and upcoming releases, please visit T.K.'s website:

www.tkleighauthor.com

PROLOGUE
END OF TEMPTATION

Julia

"Have you been following that?" the stylist asked as she cleaned her brushes.

"Sorry... What's that?"

She nodded at the screen I'd been staring at, even though I wasn't really watching. "About Lachlan Hale's sister."

I shook my head, squinting. "Who?"

"The pitcher for Atlanta," she responded, sounding shocked, as if the name were as recognizable as George Washington. "Since you're from there, I figured you'd have heard of him."

"I don't follow baseball," I offered with a smile.

"Either did I until I saw him in a uniform." She winked. "They say female attendance at games skyrockets when he's scheduled to pitch."

Curious, I stole a glance at the screen, expecting to be met with yet another tall, muscular, bearded man who did nothing for me.

Nothing could have been further from the truth.

My heart plummeted to the pit of my stomach when a pair of blue eyes stared back at me.

The same blue eyes that peered into mine as my body experienced immense pleasure all night long.

"Jules…," Naomi breathed, clutching my hand as we both gaped at the familiar man on the screen.

"They've been covering this, like, nonstop," Margo-Mary continued, completely oblivious to the utter shock rendering me mute, erasing my thoughts, stealing my breath. "Lachlan is a bit of a local legend here on the island."

I should have told her I didn't care. That I had absolutely zero interest in some young, attractive baseball player. But I couldn't find the words.

I *did* want to know more about him. About the man I knew as Chris. About the truth behind the person who'd made me smile and laugh for the first time in years. About the past we'd agreed to leave outside of our bubble.

"He went to high school here," she continued. "Was supposed to play for UCLA before Atlanta snatched him up. He started in the minors, yet quickly advanced to the majors. I'm shocked you've never heard of him. I was just in Atlanta on a film shoot. His face is all over billboards, bus stops. He's everywhere."

"We're not...," Naomi began when I simply remained mute. "We're not really into sports."

"Anyway...," Margo-Marry rattled on, lowering her voice, as if about to share a juicy piece of gossip. "A few days ago, his sister was found unresponsive in the bathtub, her wrists slit. He was the only family she had left, so he was called to identify the body. Apparently, even though she'd been diagnosed with depression, he refused to believe she'd kill herself. Punched a detective. Sent him to the hospital with a broken nose and jaw. I think there's more to the story. There had to be a reason he flew off the handle and assaulted a police officer, right?"

My breaths came quicker, heart squeezing. "Right."

He *did* say his sister had died. I'd simply assumed it was some tragic occurrence. Cancer or a car accident. But suicide? I couldn't imagine.

A flash on the screen caught my attention. My eyes involuntarily went to it. A photo of Chris...Lachlan appeared, this one of him wearing casual clothing, more closely resembling the man I'd gotten to know.

But that wasn't what caused my stomach to knot, the world spinning around me.

It was the woman at his side. His sister. The only family he had left...

And the same woman who, just last week, had confronted me, asking questions about my ex-husband.

My serial stalker, rapist, and murderer ex-husband.

My serial stalker, rapist, and murderer ex-husband she was convinced was somehow connected to more recent deaths.

It was probably nothing.

After all, Nick was in prison. Unable to hurt or manipulate anyone ever again.

Unable to stalk, rape, or kill another woman.

It was all just a coincidence that this woman who'd been looking into my ex-husband was now dead of an apparent suicide, a method he'd used on his previous victims.

A strange, unusual, unintentional coincidence.

An unbelievable, ridiculous, one-in-a-million coincidence.

Being married to a narcissistic sociopath had forced me to be observant.

To pick up on his moods before it was too late.

To learn every single detail about what made him tick, for no other reason than my own survival.

As I stared at Lachlan's sister, her eyes the same vivid blue as his, one thing I'd learned about Nick screamed at me.

When it came to him, there was no such thing as a coincidence.

CHAPTER ONE

Julia

Ten Years Ago

The crunching of tires on pavement cut through the kitchen like a shotgun, unease and trepidation filling me.

In my mind, this was just as bad as a gun going off.

Just as petrifying.

My hands grew clammy. The hairs on my nape stood on end. My pulse steadily increased, the world seeming to spin around me as I desperately tried to maintain some sort of grip on myself.

I needed to.

It was the only way to survive.

"Daddy's home," Imogene squealed, jumping up from the couch where she was surrounded by all things important to a four-year-old girl. Stuffed animals. Barbies. Coloring books. Even some play food she'd been pretending to make in her kitchen so she could grow up to be "just like Mama", as she repeatedly told me.

God, how I prayed she wouldn't. That she'd be stronger than me.

That she'd be freer than me.

Drawing in a deep, fortifying breath, I followed Imogene from the kitchen in our house on the outskirts of Charleston, glancing at the mirror by the entryway to take in my appearance. I knew Nick would be home today. Had hours to prepare for this inevitability.

It never got easier, though.

Whenever he disappeared for weeks on one of these business trips, I fantasized about vanishing myself. Taking Imogene and leaving this life behind.

Leaving *Nick* behind.

But as he reminded me every time he felt me slipping away, there was no escaping him. No matter where I'd go, he'd find me. Find us.

And he'd take Imogene from me.

So I stayed...for her.

I suffered...for her.

I died a little more every day... All for her.

When the door opened, I snapped my head toward it as Nick's frame, striking and ominous, filled the entryway.

To most, he was handsome, sexy. When I first laid eyes on him during my English 101 class my freshman year of college, I definitely thought so. Silky, blond hair. Chiseled jawline. Chestnut eyes with flecks of gold. And a smile that charmed everyone.

But there was a darkness lurking beneath his attractive exterior. I sensed it in my bones, even if I couldn't quite explain what caused it. Couldn't pinpoint my unease to one precise incident or occurrence. Instead, it was a collective premonition.

But a collective premonition, a feeling in my gut, wasn't concrete evidence.

"How are my two best girls?" he asked in his refined, Southern drawl that was as smooth as butter...and as shrewd as a snake.

It was a voice that once gave me comfort. Now all I heard was his condescension. His control.

His reminder that I belonged to him.

But was he really so bad?

Or was I simply self-sabotaging, as my therapist often suggested?

I'd heard horror stories about women who'd married controlling spouses. They weren't allowed to go out with friends. Weren't allowed to work. Weren't allowed access to their finances.

That wasn't the case with us. Nick encouraged me to spend time with my friends. That way, he wouldn't feel so bad leaving me for as long as he had to.

As far as working went, Nick had never been anything short of amazing when it came to supporting my dreams. He'd even put his own teaching and research career on hold, started working for a PR firm that dealt with educating the public on various museums, so I could start my own business.

If he were the manipulative man I often felt he was, he wouldn't do all that. Would he?

"I'm so glad you're home, Daddy!" Imogene reached her little arms toward him.

Face lighting up, Nick swooped her into his embrace, her body tiny compared to his.

I couldn't stop the smile from tugging on my lips as I watched him shower her with affection. If he were such a bad person, he wouldn't dote on our little girl the way he did.

These were the types of arguments I often had with myself, constantly at war with my thoughts. Just when I was certain there was something off about Nick, he'd do something that contradicted everything I convinced myself had to be true.

Like the time he designed a website so I could take online orders for all the baked goods I'd been making and delivering to friends up until that point, the first step in realizing my dreams of having my own bakery.

Or when he completely gutted our kitchen and had all state-of-the-art appliances installed so I could be more efficient when it came to preparing orders for my thriving business.

Or when he drove me to an empty storefront in downtown Charleston and told me he'd leased it so I'd finally have my own brick-and-mortar bakery.

Like I'd always dreamed.

If he were truly a horrible person, he wouldn't go above and beyond to do all these things for me. Would he?

Then why couldn't I shake this unsettled feeling inside me that something was off about my husband?

"And how about my wife?" Nick asked as he slowly walked toward me.

With every step he took, my heartbeat kicked up a little. Not in desire, as once happened whenever I saw him. But something I couldn't explain. Something that had grown stronger since Imogene was born.

"Is my wife happy to see me?"

I forced a smile. "Of course."

"Then show me."

I stood on my toes and pressed a chaste kiss to his lips, not lingering longer than necessary.

"Come now..." He carefully lowered Imogene to her feet. "Is that the best you can do after your husband was gone for two weeks?" There was a teasing quality to his voice. But within the frivolity and lightness, I heard something else.

A warning.

Without giving me a chance to protest, he looped his arm around my waist, pulling my body flush with his. His lips covered mine, forcing them apart, his tongue sliding against mine. His kisses once filled me with so much want. So much hunger.

Now, though, it felt forced.

Most marriages went through this kind of thing. Right? We weren't the carefree people we were before marriage and a kid. A kid who was in and out of the hospital the first year of her life. That would put a strain on any marriage. And it had. During those early days of Imogene's life, all my focus had been on her health. I never noticed Nick growing distant until he came to me in tears, confessing he'd been unfaithful.

Any other woman would have been upset.

Not me.

I was actually...relieved. Saw a way out of what I knew in my heart was a mistake.

But, somehow, I'd agreed to counseling instead.

"That's better," Nick remarked once he brought the kiss to an end.

It made me feel like he was grading me on my performance.

"Perhaps we'll try again later." He held my gaze for a beat, then turned to Imogene.

"Do you want to see what Daddy brought you?"

"Yes!" She jumped up and down, fully aware her father

never returned home empty-handed. He spoiled his little girl.

Dropping his hold on me, he went to his suitcase and rolled it into the living room. He crouched down, Imogene excitedly watching as he opened it and pulled out a square item wrapped in tissue.

"I found this in an antique store and knew you'd love it."

Pulling the tissue away, he revealed a wooden box, a dove carved on the top. From the looks of it, it appeared to be homemade. Something a father would make for a daughter. Not something easily parted with.

Turning it over, he cranked the metal key on the bottom, then lifted the top. As he did, a wooden ballerina began to twirl to the tune of "Edelweiss".

"Oh, Daddy. I love it! My very own music box. Thank you!" She flung her arms around his neck, and he squeezed her to him. When she pulled back, she took the music box and carried it over to the couch, putting some of her play beads inside it.

I took a moment to appreciate my husband's appearance as he admired our little miracle baby, his gaze awash with pride and devotion. I'd never seen a father look at their daughter with so much love.

Then again, I didn't have much to compare it to. I never knew my biological father. And my adoptive father left a lot to be desired. But my grandparents always showered me with more love than I thought I deserved. The expression on Nick's face was similar to the way my gampy would look upon me. As if his heart were so full of love, it would burst at any moment.

"And how about my beautiful wife?" Nick turned to me, expression shifting.

Less loving. More...dangerous.

"Would you like to see what I brought back for you?" His lips curved up in the corner, eyes flaming with something sinister and dark. But it was gone in a heartbeat, making me question my sanity, as always seemed to be the case.

I nodded subtly.

He advanced toward me, gripping my hip in a possessive hold. I sucked in a shaky breath at the contact. He leaned closer.

"How do you ask?"

Goosebumps prickled my skin. Most other couples would think this a fun game. A play on dominant versus submissive. But nothing about the way Nick held me felt playful. It felt...threatening.

"Please, Nick," I said, partly begging for him to let me go. Partly begging for whatever it was he brought me, even though a voice in my head told me I shouldn't want anything to do with it.

Pushing down the trepidation swimming in my stomach, I swallowed hard, brightening my expression as I forced out a charming smile.

"Can I please see what you've brought me? You always spoil us."

He crushed his lips to mine. I moaned, playing the part of his affectionate, loving wife, even though everything about this felt...wrong.

But I had no proof. He'd never hit me. Never hurt me. In fact, he did everything to give me my dreams at the expense of his own.

"Because you're my Hera," he murmured against my lips. "My goddess. My queen. My eternal beloved." He trailed kisses along my jawline before pressing his mouth back to mine.

When he finally pulled away, much to my relief, he kept his eyes trained on mine. Reaching into the inside pocket of his tweed jacket, he removed a long, gold chain, a tulip dangling from the end, the bulb a pear-shaped opal. The gold appeared tarnished and worn. This definitely wasn't something he'd found at the corner jewelry store.

"When I saw this, I knew there was only one neck on this planet it would look good on." He stepped behind me, brushing my long, blonde waves off my shoulders.

I remained frozen as he secured the piece. It was delicate, weighing mere ounces. But it felt so heavy around my neck, suffocating and cutting off my air.

I had no reason to believe this was anything but a generous gift from a doting husband.

But, somehow, I sensed there was more to it.

That he simply didn't walk into an antique store and purchase this.

That there was something incredibly malevolent about how he came to be the owner of this necklace.

I wanted it off me. Wanted nothing to do with it.

But I didn't have a choice.

With Nick, I never had a choice.

CHAPTER TWO

Julia

Present Day

I stared ahead, consumed by my thoughts. My memories.

My fear.

It was back, coiling through me, wrapping around my lungs and heart, cutting off my ability to breathe, to think, to survive as I tried to process everything I'd learned in the past few minutes.

The man I'd been sleeping with lost his sister to suicide. The same woman who, mere days ago, had approached me when I was out to lunch with my daughter, insisting my ex-husband was responsible for more recent deaths.

The same woman who, hours later, was found dead of an apparent suicide, a method my ex-husband was known for.

Even admired for by some.

I kept telling myself it was impossible. That Nick was in prison. That he'd spend the rest of his life in an orange jumpsuit, only allowed an hour of fresh air a day.

It was better than he deserved.

He'd left a trail of dead women in his wake, something that could have been avoided had I simply opened my eyes and saw what my gut had tried to force me to for years.

But that was the thing about being married to a master manipulator. It was impossible to pinpoint the moment it all started because you were unaware anything was happening until the truth became unavoidable.

You were married to a monster.

On the outside, Nick was this charismatic, charming man everyone respected and admired. Handsome. Exceedingly intelligent. And just an all-around good person.

But his soul was as black as a starless night.

This was a man who often fixated on a woman for something as small as a kind smile. Who stalked his prey for months. Who raped her, then continued stalking her, breaking into her home, the one place she felt safe. Who *wanted* her to know he'd been there, often moving things around. A coffee mug here. Opening a window there. All to make her feel like she was losing her mind. To make her *friends* think she wasn't doing well mentally. He'd observe her downward spiral with a sick sense of excitement, manipulating her until he watched her take her final breath.

He was smart. Chose his victims wisely, never targeting two women in the same jurisdiction for fear the police would catch on. Not that they would. After all, his victims died of "suicide", a fact the authorities were certain of.

Until I found his journals detailing the stalking, as well as the keepsake boxes containing all the souvenirs he'd kept.

Well, not *all* the souvenirs.

He liked sharing them.

I just didn't know it at the time.

But now I did. The mere memory of Nick draping me in jewelry that had been removed from a dead woman's body made my stomach churn, my skin growing cold.

I tried to find comfort in the fact that he wasn't a serial killer when I married him. Or even a serial rapist, although many would argue differently. Most considered me one of his first rape victims.

And I would have been one of his murder victims, too, if I hadn't found the courage to break free from his years of grooming and manipulation.

"Jules."

Naomi's voice cut through my thoughts, returning me to the present, reminding me I was free. That I never had to see Nick again.

I tore my gaze to my left where my best friend sat,

clutching my hand, concerned eyes studying my every move.

"It's okay." She dropped her voice to no louder than a whisper. "It's nothing. Just because that woman died of suicide doesn't mean anything." She leaned closer. "Nick's in prison. Where he'll eventually die. He will never be released. Hell, for all we know, he's received a taste of his own medicine and spends his days as some badass prisoner's fuck toy."

Any other day, I would have found amusement in her suggestion. Not today.

"That's not it, Naomi. It's not just the scenario. It's…" I trailed off, shaking my head, searching for the words to tell her just how closely related this revelation truly was. Something I couldn't do with the hair and makeup artist from the morning news show I was about to appear on hovering nearby.

As if picking up on the reason for my hesitation, Naomi glanced over her shoulder. "Hey, Margo?"

The blonde tore her eyes from the television as a reporter talked about Lachlan's connection to the island. How this was where he'd gotten his start in professional baseball, thanks to his high school coach inviting recruiters out here. "Yeah?"

"Can you give us a minute?"

"Sure." Smacking her gum, she left the room, completely oblivious to the tension growing thicker with every passing moment.

When the door closed, Naomi refocused her attention on me. "Okay. What's up? It's not just Nick, is it?"

I slowly shook my head. "That woman... Claire. A few days ago, she came up to me as Imogene and I were having lunch."

This certainly got Naomi's attention. She straightened, then leaned toward me. "What did she say?"

I swallowed hard. "It all happened so quickly. One second, I was having an enjoyable lunch with Imogene before she left for camp. The next, this woman bullied her way into our conversation, shoved a voice recorder in front of me, claiming to host a podcast, and asked me to comment on a handful of recent suicides she alleged were related to Nick."

"What did you say?"

"What do you think? I just..." I blinked back the tears threatening at the possibility that, had I been a bit more understanding, a bit more receptive, perhaps I could have prevented her death.

Now I had even more blood on my already stained hands.

Why didn't I at least talk to her? Listen to what she had to say?

Instead, I'd asked that she be removed, as I did whenever some true crime fanatic sought me out.

In the months following Nick's arrest, my bakeries were inundated with obsessed fans hoping to get a photo taken with me. The wife of the notorious "Professor", as he'd been dubbed in the media.

Thankfully, that had all died down over the years, apart from the occasional fanatic or, worse, true crime podcaster wanting to revisit Nick's crimes.

Which I thought Claire was.

When she suggested Nick was involved in even more deaths, and in front of a wide-eyed Imogene, I had no choice but to turn her away, refuse to answer her questions. I couldn't. My daughter had been traumatized enough, reporters constantly begging to do a story about her. Probably wondering if she were as psychotic as Nick simply because she had the same DNA.

I just wanted to put the past behind us.

I feared I'd never be able to.

"When the truth came out and my world became a media circus," I explained, "I made a promise to myself that I would never put Imogene in danger again. That I would do everything in my power to protect her. To keep her safe, no matter the price I was forced to pay."

Naomi squeezed my hand, giving me a reassuring smile. "And you have. You did what any mother would do in that situation. Protect your child at all costs. I may not have any kids...hell, I've never even been in a relationship long enough to entertain the notion...but I love Imogene as if she were my own. I would have done the same thing. So stop blaming yourself for what happened to that poor girl. You are not at fault here. I know you blamed yourself for what Nick did to those women. But as was the case all those years ago, too, *he* was at fault. Not you. Just like you're not responsible for this, either."

"Easy for you to say," I mumbled. "You didn't essentially tell Claire to fuck off without so much as listening to what proof she had." I drew in a long breath, all the inexplicable feelings of guilt and shame that followed me throughout my marriage to Nick returning.

If they had ever left.

The jury was still out on that.

"Well, at least we know one thing for certain," I said in a chipper voice, resecuring the mask I'd worn for years.

Naomi gave me a quizzical look. "What's that?"

"Think about it." I subtly nodded toward the screen where a shampoo commercial now played. "It makes sense. I'd repeatedly questioned what he could possibly see in me." I smiled sadly, doing my best to hide the hurt in my voice over the realization. "Now I know."

Naomi studied me for a beat, brows furrowed, attempting to put the pieces together. Her eyes soon widened before her expression hardened.

"Don't you dare," she snipped, finger in my face. "Don't even go there. You're wrong, Julia Blaire Prescott. I saw the way he looked at you. There's no way he faked that just to get information." She shook her head, collecting her thoughts. Then she leaned toward me. "I felt it in my soul."

I paused, considering her words. Then I hung my head, resigned. "You may have felt it in your soul, and maybe there's a part of me that wants to believe it, too. But I need to be rational about this. Have to look at the facts."

"And what are the 'facts'?" she asked, using air quotes.

I held my head high, smoothing a hand down my dress as I slid off the stool, squaring my shoulders. "That I'm a forty-year-old woman, and he's a ridiculously attractive professional baseball player who's probably slept with models and actresses. Let's not even talk about all the effort I made him go through to get laid." I barked out a laugh, throwing my hands up in frustration. "I made him bake a fucking cake, for crying out loud."

"A...cake?" Naomi furrowed her brows. "What do you mean?"

I waved her off. "That's beside the point."

"Then what *is* the point, Julia?" She stood and gripped my biceps. "You're letting Nick into your head again. You—"

I pulled out of her hold. "The point is that no horny, young guy would go through all that for a piece of ass unless there's something else in it for him." I leaned toward her. "Unless he *needs* something else from it. He knows. That's the only explanation." I crossed my arms in front of my chest, pretending the idea that Chris...Lachlan led me on to get information didn't gut me like it did.

"Knows what?"

"Everything! He knows who I am. Knew his sister came to see me. And he knew all he had to do was turn on the charm and I'd fall under his spell. Just like I did with Nick."

With every word I spoke, my voice grew louder and more irritable.

"*That's* why he agreed to my proposal. Not because he wanted to spend the week with me. But because he figured I might tell him what I refused to tell his sister."

Naomi stared at me, jaw agape, silence ringing in the space between us.

A knock suddenly reverberated in the room, cutting through the truth clinging to the air like the foul stench of death and decay.

"Ms. Prescott. Five minutes."

"I'll be right there," I said with a saccharine smile, despite the fact the stage manager couldn't see me. It was a trick I'd learned years ago. Whenever shit got bad, just plaster a smile onto your face. If you smiled, you'd sound happier. For years, it was the only way I could hide the truth that I felt like a prisoner in my marriage.

"You can't really believe that, Jules," Naomi said once we heard the sound of retreating footsteps.

I avoided her gaze, walking to the mirror and taking a few seconds to ensure my makeup hid all evidence of my emotions, transitioning into the Julia Prescott America had grown to love.

The Julia Prescott my PR firm insisted I needed to become in order to protect my business from ruin. To do everything I could to separate myself from Nick's actions.

"It's too much of a coincidence to believe otherwise. If being married to Nick taught me anything, it's that there's no such thing as a coincidence. Not where he's concerned."

"And if your marriage to Nick taught *me* anything..." Naomi touched my forearm, turning me toward her, "it's that he's always had the uncanny ability to get into your head and under your skin."

"This isn't him getting into my head. This is merely a determination based on facts. Not *his* interpretation of the facts. Mine, and mine alone."

"No." A sad smile tugged on her lips. "It's an assumption. I'm not saying you're wrong. You could very well be right. I won't deny it is...remarkable. But not everyone has ulterior motives. Not everyone is the bad guy. Not everyone is like your ex-husband." She allowed her statement to linger for a moment before brightening her expression. "For all you know, this could just be a messed-up twist of fate."

"Twist of fate?"

"Exactly." She clutched my hands in hers. "Two lost souls whose connection runs deeper than the physical. Maybe there's a reason your paths crossed. Maybe there's something bigger at play. The universe forcing you together so you both can finally move on from your pasts." She smirked. "*And* to give you a week of sinful, lust-filled, depraved fucking you most certainly deserve."

I stared at her for several moments. The tension too much for me, I threw my head back and laughed. That was one of the reasons I loved Naomi. Why I needed her in my life. Through it all, she'd been my voice of reason. The one person who had no problem calling me out for my shit. The one person who reminded me what was truth and what was just Nick's manipulation still at play, even all these years later.

"Several-orgasms-a-night sinful, lust-filled, depraved fucking," I reminded her, my tone light.

"Stop rubbing it in, will ya?" She flashed a smile before her expression grew serious once more. "Please don't do anything rash because one asshole taught you to assume the worst of everyone. Promise you'll talk to Lachlan first. See what he has to say about it all. And make sure you actually *listen* to him. This could very well come as a huge shock to him, too."

I wanted to remind her that listening to Nick didn't exactly turn out all that great for me. But I didn't, nodding instead. "Okay. Promise."

"Good." She seemed appeased by that. But I wasn't.

She may have thought it all just a big coincidence.

I knew better, though.

Nothing in life was truly a coincidence. Not when Nick was involved.

CHAPTER THREE

Lachlan

The calming sounds of the ocean surrounded me as I bobbed on my surfboard, studying the swells for the right wave to ride to shore.

After Nikko's phone call this morning, I couldn't stop thinking about what he'd found out about that name — Lucretia. I didn't want to believe the story about Lucretia being raped, then taking her own life had anything to do with what happened to Claire. It was bad enough I felt in my heart she'd been murdered and the police didn't want to investigate. The idea she might have been assaulted, just like Piper, tore me apart, my anger overwhelming me.

So instead of doing something I knew I'd regret, I sought comfort on the ocean waves. Hoped being out here would give me some sort of clarity. Some sort of direction.

Spotting a wave forming in the distance, I readied myself, gripping the board. Just as it approached, I hoisted myself to my feet, fighting to keep my balance. As I caught the wave, leaning into it, instinct kicked in. Piper always said surfing was a lot like riding a bike. Once you learned, you never forgot how to do it. The memory brought a smile to my face, and for a split second, I almost felt her out here, reassuring me I was on the right path, as she often did during her life.

I would have been lying if I claimed things with her were always good. That her decision to cheat came out of left field.

But it didn't.

We were so young. At the time of her death, I was only twenty-two, she a year younger. It didn't help we were both stubborn and opinionated. Suffice it to say, we had our fair share of arguments.

But when things were good, they were great.

Then again, I wasn't exactly around much. We'd only been dating six months when I received the phone call that changed the direction of my life. I'd planned to attend UCLA, so we already knew we'd have to deal with a long-distance relationship.

But signing with Atlanta meant being a nine-hour flight away instead of only five. Not to mention living in whatever housing the team put me up in.

So instead of having the summer to spend as much time together as we could before I moved into my dorm in

Southern California, I had mere hours after my high school graduation before I had to board a plane to embark on my dream of playing professional baseball, even if it was only the minors. Everyone had to start somewhere.

In the beginning, we did everything to make it work. Since she was in her senior year of high school, our time together was limited. We FaceTimed as much as possible, though. And when she could, she came out to see me play. But considering I lived with five other players in a tiny apartment, anytime she contemplated coming out, we had to take into account the expense of getting a hotel room, something we weren't always able to do, since minor league players didn't exactly rake in the big bucks. The only reason I could support myself at all after my mum died less than a year into my career was because, thanks to Nikko's advice, I invested my inheritance into a house with an in-law apartment I could turn into a beach rental. If I hadn't, I doubted I would have been able to sustain playing in the minors *and* coming home to visit as often as I did.

But as time went on, the distance certainly took its toll. We fought more. FaceTimed less. I felt her slipping from me, yet did nothing to reel her back in. I guess I assumed she'd always be there.

I should have known better.

Should have tried harder.

Should have cared more.

Her cheating definitely wasn't right. But I understood why she did it. I wasn't there for her. Didn't appreciate her.

Even when I was physically present, I wasn't mentally present. I never gave her my full attention, every thought focused on advancing to the next level of my career.

Looking back on all the arguments and frustration, I realized our relationship actually ended the second I left Hawaii to pursue my baseball career. We just didn't want to admit it to ourselves.

As I reached the shore, I hopped off my board, unclipping myself from the tether before wading through the shallows. The mid-morning sun beamed down on the sand, the beach becoming increasingly populated with tourists who hoped to find a more peaceful area than you'd typically find around Waikiki.

Board in hand, I jogged up the beach and toward my mum's old house, resting the surfboard against the brick privacy wall. I unzipped my wetsuit as I continued toward the house, coming to an abrupt stop when I noticed a figure sitting on the bench in Claire's garden.

Reacting quickly, I grabbed the first thing I could get my hands on — a baseball bat.

"You have exactly ten seconds to tell me who you are and what the fuck you're doing on my property before I use your head for batting practice."

The figure jumped to his feet, whirling around, eyes wide. "I'm so sorry. I didn't—"

"Who are you?" I demanded.

"My name's... My name's Ethan."

"Okay, *Ethan*." I gripped the bat, stepping toward him.

He tensed even more, hands held in front of him in surrender.

Truth be told, he wasn't even remotely intimidating. He was tall and lanky, his blond hair perfectly groomed. His pale skin made me question whether he'd been exposed to any sunlight recently. He had a youthful appearance and couldn't have been any older than thirty.

"Tell me what you're doing here. Unless you want the seagulls to feast on your brain for lunch."

"I... I..."

"Answer me," I ordered. "Five seconds..." I inched closer, tightening my grip.

"I'm a friend of Claire's!" he shouted, face scrunching up, eyes closed, fully preparing himself for the first hit. "And I think I may know why she was murdered!"

I blinked, his statement taking me by surprise. But I didn't relax my posture. Not until I had more answers. Not until I knew this wasn't a ploy.

"But she committed suicide," I stated, playing devil's advocate.

He slowly opened one eye, then the other, relaxing slightly when I didn't advance. "Come on." He gave me a knowing look. "You don't believe that. I heard about your arrest. How you punched a detective because they refused to look into her death, insisting it was suicide."

"The police made their determination," I argued noncommittally.

I had my reasons for knowing Claire would never take

her own life. But what about this person I'd never heard my sister mention? How could I believe he actually knew her?

Then again, we didn't exactly talk that much in the months before her death. Not like we once did. I had no idea what was going on in her life.

"If it were a suicide, why would they confiscate her laptop and cell phone?" Ethan interjected.

I relaxed my grip on the bat, yet kept it in my hands. I'd been wondering the same thing.

"It's because she didn't kill herself," he continued. "And because the police knew she was on to something."

"Like what?"

"Something for the podcast."

I blinked repeatedly. "What podcast?"

"Your sister's podcast." His brows furrowed in confusion. "She never told you about it?"

"I... No, she didn't." A weight settled on my chest as renewed feelings of guilt washed over me.

I thought we had a good relationship. Once cancer took our mum from us just weeks after Claire graduated high school, we were all each other had.

Now I feared I didn't know my sister like I thought I did. That I'd allowed my anger to come between me and the only family I had left.

And now she was gone.

"She probably just figured you were so busy with your career you wouldn't care about her podcast."

"I was never too busy for Claire," I murmured, although my voice lacked conviction.

Ethan offered me a half-smile. Even this complete stranger probably sensed I was full of crap.

The truth was, even if I weren't too busy, I didn't exactly let her know that. Particularly these past few months when I avoided her phone calls, my only communication in the form of a quick text telling her I was busy and that we'd catch up soon.

That day never came.

All because I didn't want to admit she may have been right.

Didn't want to consider the possibility that the person who broke into my home and assaulted Piper was still out there.

"What kind of podcast?" I asked past the lump in my throat.

"True crime."

I laughed to myself. I should have known.

Throughout high school, Claire spent quite a bit of time with our neighbor, Mrs. Young, who was notorious for her obsession with true crime. Apparently, she passed that on to my sister.

"It was pretty popular," Ethan continued. "It's how we met. She needed help researching some of the topics she covered on her show. I used to be a fraud investigator for insurance companies."

"Sounds thrilling."

He snorted at the sarcasm in my voice. "Not really. Which was why I was more than eager to help Claire. Do something more exciting than track down an antique piece of jewelry some rich asshole claimed was stolen, only to learn he'd sold it on the black market. For all the money those pricks have, you'd think they'd be able to afford the sense to not make it so easy to catch them committing a crime. But if they were, I'd be out of a job." He laughed nervously.

"So... This podcast... You said she was working on something for it?"

"I tried to tell her not to. That it wasn't worth it. But when Claire made up her mind, no one could convince her to back down."

A nostalgic smile lifted my lips. I knew that all too well. "You're right about that." I stared into the distance for a moment, then returned my hardened expression to his. "So what *was* she working on?"

"It all started about four or five months ago. People often wrote to the show with requests of topics they'd like her to cover. If she got enough of the same one, she'd look into it. While researching one of these requests, she was convinced she found a connection to what happened to Piper, your ex-girlfriend."

"I know who Piper is," I barked out.

"Of course you do. I just..."

He glanced at the bat still in my hand. "Do you mind

putting that down? I've seen what you can do with the right pitch, and it's kind of freaking me out."

I hesitated, then relented, leaning the bat against the bench. "One wrong move, and I pick it back up."

"Not to worry. I want justice for Claire, just like you do."

Content with his assurance, I nodded, crossing my arms in front of my chest. "Tell me about this case she was looking into."

He shook his head. "Probably one of the creepiest fuckers we ever covered on the show. Not because he was this brutal serial killer who inflicted intense bodily harm on his victims, but because he'd managed to kill each of his victims by proxy."

"Proxy?" I scrunched my brows, dropping my arms. "What the bloody hell does that mean? He hired someone? Doesn't that defeat the purpose of being a serial killer? Aren't they supposed to get off on killing or something?"

"No. He didn't hire anyone. But every single one of his victims died by taking their own lives."

My heart plummeted to the pit of my stomach, a chill washing over me as I recalled the story of Lucretia.

"That's why he's often considered one of the most depraved killers in recent history. He was able to get inside his victims' heads to the point they were convinced the only way to escape was—"

"To take their own lives."

"Exactly. The media dubbed him 'The Professor',

because he was a highly intelligent college professor with a handful of PhDs to his name. But after researching, learning he'd rape his victims in the hopes of them eventually taking their own lives, your sister came up with a better nickname for him. A more fitting nickname."

"What's that?" I asked, pulse increasing, face heating as dread settled low in my stomach.

"'The Lucretia Killer.'"

CHAPTER FOUR

Lachlan

Ethan's words echoed around me, cutting above the ocean waves crashing in the distance. There was no way this was merely a coincidence. It couldn't be.

Leaning toward Ethan, I glowered at him. "Tell me everything about this so-called 'Lucretia Killer'. *Now.*"

He jumped, body going rigid. "O-of course." He nodded toward the patio set on the lanai. "Do you mind if we sit?"

I glared at him for a beat. I didn't find him threatening. Hell, I was pretty sure my accountant was more intimidating than he was. That seemed to be Claire's type, though. Tall, lanky, highly intelligent. She was definitely a "brains over brawn" kind of girl.

I gave him a terse nod. Exhaling a relieved breath, he

grabbed a leather messenger bag off the ground and slung it over his shoulder before timidly walking toward the patio set. He waited for me to sit in one of the chairs before lowering himself onto the wicker couch across from me, nervously rubbing his hands along his khaki pants.

When he didn't say anything, I raised a brow. "So, this 'Lucretia Killer'..."

"Right." He parted his lips, then hesitated. "Would you rather Claire tell you about him?"

I tilted my head. "Excuse me?"

"Her podcast. You could—"

I held up my hand, stopping him.

While part of me wanted to listen to her podcast to see what she'd been up to, I didn't think I could put myself through that. Not yet. Hell, listening to Claire's voicemail repeatedly while answering the detective's questions was what pushed me to my breaking point, leading me to throwing a few punches. I couldn't stomach listening to an entire podcast, her voice reminding me that I'd turned my back on her and she was dead because of it.

Because of me.

"Not yet." I swallowed hard. "I... I can't."

He gave me a sad, sympathetic smile. "I haven't been able to listen to any of her podcasts, either. She'd recorded one for this week that I was supposed to go through and edit, but I haven't. Hell, I haven't even told her listeners she died."

"I'm sure they already know. It's been all over the news."

"No one knew her by Claire Hale. She used a different name. Claire DeLune. A play on the Debussy song."

I laughed slightly under my breath. "That was what our mum always called her. Mum was an accomplished pianist. Classically trained. So when Claire was born during a full moon, and since *clair de lune* is French for moonlight—"

"She named her Claire. I know." He held my gaze for a beat, then cleared his throat. "So, 'The Lucretia Killer'..."

"Right."

I pushed down the emotions bubbling to the surface the best I could, focusing on Ethan in the hopes of figuring out what the hell was going on.

Get Claire the justice she deserved.

"His real name is Domenic Jaskulski. Like I said, he's probably the most notorious proxy serial killer in the history of serial killers."

"Because he killed his victims without ever actually killing them himself," I clarified.

"Correct. This guy is a genius. A certifiable genius. There's not a lot of information about his younger years. Grew up in foster care. Graduated high school at thirteen. Had a couple bachelor's degrees by the time he turned fifteen. His first master's at seventeen. That's the kind of intelligence we're talking about here."

"Impressive."

"Too bad all that intelligence turned him into a narcissistic sociopath," he scoffed. "Now Domenic, who usually went by Nick, didn't start his criminal career by killing. As is typically the case, it began with stalking. But being the intellectual he was, it wasn't just following and watching, like most stalkers. He always wrote down his observations about the women he stalked. And that stalking soon graduated to rape."

"Let me guess," I interjected. "Rape eventually turned into murder."

I'd listened to enough of Mrs. Young's stories about serial killers to be familiar with the progression from a young boy who abused animals to a disturbed man who got off on torturing humans.

"Yes. And we can thank a woman by the name of Annabelle Landry for that."

"Who was she?"

"Nick was a humanities professor at various colleges all along the East Coast. Annabelle Landry had the misfortune of being enrolled in a Shakespeare class Nick taught at a college in Charleston. Her friends described her as outgoing. Always happy. Smart. Constantly giving back to the community. She was a model student."

Ethan leaned toward me, arms resting on his knees, expression animated. It was obvious he was quite passionate about this.

"Keep in mind that Nick's brain is wired differently from ours. While the rest of us see a kind smile as just a friendly gesture, he saw it as something more. An invitation.

"So Nick cracked open a journal and got to work writing down everything he observed about Annabelle. What she ate. What she wore. Boyfriends. Friends. Favorite TV shows. *Everything.*

"When he knew she wasn't home, he broke into her apartment. Went through her drawers. Stole her underwear. Removed strands of hair from her brush. And he put it all into a keepsake box, probably in the hopes the trinkets alone would be enough to satisfy his...urges."

"Jesus Christ," I muttered, stomach churning in repulsion.

"As the semester wore on, Nick's obsession with Annabelle grew. One night, he watched her while she was out at a bar with her friends for trivia night, something Nick observed her going to every week. Now, Annabelle was from a very conservative, religious family. Went on mission trips. Did volunteer work with a homebuilding organization. Stuff like that.

"Unfortunately, Annabelle wasn't feeling well that night and left early. Her friends offered to leave with her, make sure she got home okay, but her apartment was only a few blocks away. She insisted she'd be fine. Unbeknownst to her, Nick followed her, watched as she wavered on her feet. She was so unsteady that when she finally made it into her apartment, she didn't even bother locking the door before collapsing onto the couch. I'll give you one guess who took advantage of that."

"He drugged her at the bar, didn't he?" I remarked, glancing up at Ethan. "Just so he could rape her."

Ethan nodded. "But that's not the worst of it."

"It's not?"

"In the aftermath of that night, Annabelle struggled, something Nick took great joy in as he wrote down his observations in his journal. She obviously knew something had happened. She woke up sore in places that shouldn't have been sore. Blood in places that shouldn't have been bleeding."

"Did she go to the police?"

Ethan slowly shook his head. "No."

"Why not?"

"I surmise the same reason any number of women don't report being sexually assaulted, even if fully aware of what had happened, which Annabelle wasn't. Rape is a crime of personal nature. Reporting it means having to relive it all over again. Not to mention, the police are sometimes in the habit of blaming the victim."

I clenched my fists. I'd witnessed a woman being raped, and it was the worst thing I'd ever seen. I understood why most were hesitant to come forward. *I* didn't like answering questions after what happened to Piper. And I wasn't the one who was violated in such a perverse and inhumane way.

"So, instead of reporting it, Annabelle kept it to

herself," Ethan continued. "She wasn't sure what had happened in the first place, so what was she going to do? Tell the police she *might* have been raped?

"Over the next several weeks, she spiraled downward. Withdrew from friends. Distanced herself from family. Unfortunately for Annabelle, Nick had a front-row seat to her transition from a once vibrant woman to a shell of a person. And being the manipulative prick he is, he decided to mess with her head even more.

"He walked into class one day and announced that he'd made a change to the syllabus. Instructed them that instead of studying *Othello*, they'd be squeezing in two of Shakespeare's epic poems — *Venus and Adonis*, and *The Rape of Lucrece*."

Ethan lifted his gaze to mine. "Do you know the story about the *Rape of Lucrece*? Or Lucretia?"

I slowly nodded. "Nikko, one of my good friends, has been looking into Claire's death. She'd left a voicemail mentioning that name. After doing a bit of research, he uncovered the story about the Roman noblewoman who refused the prince's advances, so he raped her. Since she was dishonored, she threw herself on the mercy of her husband and father, pleading for revenge, before stabbing herself."

"That about sums it up."

"So Nick not only raped Annabelle, he forced her to read about another woman who suffered the same fate, then killed herself."

"Twisted, right?"

"That may be the understatement of the year."

"Now, at this point, it didn't appear Nick intentionally did this so she'd follow in Lucretia's footsteps. It was more of a mind game. And he loved to play mind games. However, mere days later, news spread around campus."

"She'd committed suicide," I stated evenly.

"Yup. But get this... During Nick's next class, you'd think he'd forego the lecture on *The Rape of Lucrece*, given the subject matter and the fact they'd just lost a classmate to suicide."

"He didn't?" I arched a brow, my voice heavy with disbelief, although nothing should have surprised me about this guy.

"Nope. He held the lecture, going on and on about how beautiful Lucretia's death was. How *noble* it was. How *freeing* it was. People left his class in tears, yet the fucker just kept talking."

"Jesus." A chill washed down my spine at the depravity and lack of compassion. Then again, he *was* a serial killer. A severe lack of empathy was probably a requirement.

"After Annabelle's suicide, something apparently sparked inside Nick," Ethan continued. "He's a textbook example of a true predator, a sadistic rapist. He learned how to get inside his victims' heads to create the desired outcome. In Nick's case, it was manipulation, domination, and control. He was charming enough to win over any woman one minute, desperate for power and control over her the next.

"He didn't immediately set out to manipulate another woman to commit suicide. Over the next few years, he simply returned to his typical MO of stalking and rape. But it was no longer enough. Not now that he'd gotten a taste of ultimate power. So, after two years of chasing that high and falling short, he came up with a new plan."

"Which was?" I asked, not sure I wanted to know.

"Using an alias, he sought out women who were already vulnerable, attending group self-help meetings for those struggling with depression. When he found the perfect subject, so to speak, he did what he did best."

"Stalked them."

"Exactly. Researched everything about them. Their hopes. Their dreams. Their fears. Being in the same self-help group allowed him access to information he normally wouldn't have been privy to. As with Annabelle, he broke into their homes, stole things. Then, when the moment was right, he attacked, drugging and raping them.

"As if raping a woman already suffering from depression weren't enough, he continued breaking into their homes. Moved stuff around. Left gifts, sometimes photos he'd taken of them without their knowledge. Even turned on the stove. All things that made them question their sanity until they couldn't stand it anymore and took their own life. It had almost become a game for him. See how little it took for him to weasel his way into their brains and coerce them into ending their life. And he never failed. Every woman he set his sights on eventually killed herself."

"Jesus," I murmured again, everything about this guy giving me the creeps. What kind of depraved human intentionally stalked someone who already felt vulnerable, then exerted their power and control just to get off on watching them die?

"What you have to understand about this guy's psychological makeup is that it wasn't about the rape or murder."

"It was about the control," I stated.

"Exactly."

"Did he ever get caught? He's not still out there, is he?" I assumed Ethan and Claire wouldn't know everything they did about him if it were still an unsolved crime.

"He's currently spending the rest of his life as a resident of the Georgia Department of Corrections."

I sat in silence for several seconds, a sickening feeling in my stomach. I'd heard my fair share of deranged stories, thanks to Mrs. Young's obsession with true crime. But the story Ethan just shared was by far one of the creepiest, if for no other reason than this guy's ability to get into his victim's head to the point that he could coerce them to kill themselves.

As if the world weren't twisted enough.

"It's an...interesting story." I licked my lips, scrunching my brows. "But what does this have to do with what happened to Piper?" I leaned toward him. "She didn't kill herself. She—"

"When Claire was doing her research into all the victims, something she insisted on doing to properly tell their story and not simply glorify what the bastard did, she noticed a similarity. Domenic Jaskulski's second victim was Evelyn Price, a social media influencer who died July tenth. Piper's date of death was also July tenth, correct? And wasn't she also a social media influencer for a variety of surf brands?"

"Yeah, but—"

"His first victim was Annabelle Landry."

I nodded. "I remember."

He opened the flap of his messenger bag and pulled out a large stack of files. He placed them on the coffee table and grabbed the top one, opening it to a photo of a smiling, young brunette, setting it in front of me.

"This is Autumn Quinn. A college student who volunteered for a homebuilding organization, much like Annabelle Landry. Five years ago this past spring, she also died of suicide on March third. The same date as Ms. Landry."

I blinked, still not entirely convinced. It was somewhat suspicious. But it could have been a coincidence, too.

Grabbing another file, he threw yet another photo in front of me. "This is Lilian King."

"Let me guess. College student. Volunteered for a homebuilding organization. Died March third."

He nodded. "Three years ago."

He threw one last photo onto the pile. "Everly Flores. Four months ago. This is what Claire figured out."

"What is?"

He leveled a stare on me. "Someone's repeating Domenic Jaskulski's kill cycle."

CHAPTER
FIVE

Lachlan

"So...a copycat?" I asked Ethan after taking a moment to process his theory.

"Not exactly. A copycat would mimic the original offender. This doesn't read like a copycat to me. It didn't to Claire, either. This guy isn't trying to replicate the crimes. If he were, he'd stalk his victims, rape them, then try to get them to take their own lives.

"This new guy, while arguably intelligent enough to evade detection, is not as...calculating. It's more like a tribute that borders on obsession. Something he absolutely must do, no matter what. On March third, he *has* to kill a college student who also volunteers her time to a home-building charity. *Has* to kill a social media influencer on July tenth." He tossed another file in front of me, *Evelyn*

Price written on the tab. "*Has* to kill a hotel desk clerk on October thirteenth." Another folder. "A flight attendant January twenty-ninth." Another. "A barista April fourth." Another. "A personal trainer August twelfth." Another. "A waitress and aspiring model on December thirtieth. Then he starts the cycle all over again."

I stare at the folders. "Did Claire ever go to the police with this?"

He blows out a laugh under his breath. "Of course she did. But no one would listen. Insisted it was all a 'coincidence'. Not to mention, each of these deaths, like with Domenic Jaskulski, was ruled a suicide. But unlike with Nick, we're pretty certain these women didn't take their own lives. That this guy made sure they died on the right day. Which was why she believed he didn't abort his mission when he realized Piper wasn't alone, as he'd originally hoped. He *needs* to complete the ritual. It isn't just a hope or desire, but something he needs to fulfill. So when he broke into your house and saw you there, he had to do everything in his power to ensure he completed the ritual, no matter the cost."

I scrubbed a hand over my face, all too aware of the cost incurred that night. Claire almost didn't survive, and I was lucky team management was understanding. I'd just been promoted to the majors, then was brutally attacked hours later, resulting in a serious concussion and a fractured knee cap, an injury that put me on the disabled list for the rest of the season. But through it all, I was determined to come back stronger than ever. To prove I belonged in the majors. Which was precisely what I did.

"Did she at least talk to Nikko about this?" I asked. "He's a detective and close family friend. Practically like a brother to me. And her."

"She told me about him and his background. She wanted to gather more information before dragging him into this, considering who Piper was to him. That's why she hoped to talk to his wife."

"Whose wife?"

"Domenic Jaskulski's. Well, I suppose *ex*-wife is the more appropriate term."

My eyes widened. "He was married?"

"And had a daughter. It's actually fairly common among serial killers to live a double life. If he were this uneducated loner who worked a menial job, he'd be on law enforcement's radar. He'd at least fit the profile. But an educated family man with a career who was regarded as a pillar of the community? Not exactly the type of person who comes to mind when hearing about this kind of thing, is it?"

"Definitely not. Did the wife know what he was doing?"

"There's a difference of opinion on that. But based on the evidence that came out during his trial, it was determined she was probably one of his very first victims."

I nodded, staring into the distance, the sound of children laughing as they played on the beach like a perverse soundtrack to the twisted story I'd just heard.

"Why did Claire want to talk to this guy's wife? What did she hope she'd be able to tell her?"

"Claire wanted to see if Julia knew who could be doing something like this. And to see if her theory was correct."

"And what theory was that?"

"This guy…" He gestured to the photos of dozens of women laid out on the coffee table. "He's methodic. Ritualistic. At least that's the profile we constructed based on the little information we were able to get from friends and family members of the victims. Do you want to know what every single one told us?"

"What's that?"

"Each mentioned an important piece of jewelry was missing. Something they never would have parted with. Something meaningful." He paused, slowly lifting his eyes to mine. "Was there anything of Piper's you noticed missing after she died?"

My pulse steadily increased as I nodded. "A necklace. Something I had made for her after she won her first big surfing tournament. After she died, I wanted to do something with it as a memorial to her, but I was never able to find it."

"Claire believed this was intentional. Part of the ritual. While Nick routinely stole things from his victims as he stalked them, on the day they committed suicide, he always took one more memento."

"What was that?" I asked hesitantly, not sure I wanted to know.

"A souvenir to commemorate their death. Always a meaningful piece of jewelry, which he would then gift to his wife."

"And Claire believed whoever's repeating his kill cycle is also giving his wife the jewelry?"

"Not the perpetrator's wife. But Nick's ex. It was just a theory, but Claire hoped if she could confirm whether the ex-wife had received any odd gifts after Nick went to prison, it might be all the proof she needed to unequivocally show there was something going on. That it was more than a mere coincidence a waitress happened to take her life on the same date as the waitress did in Jaskulski's case."

"And what did she say?"

"Who?"

"The ex-wife. What was her name?"

"Julia Prescott."

"What did Julia tell Claire?"

Ethan shrugged. "No idea. The last time I spoke with Claire, she told me she'd followed Julia to a restaurant and planned to confront her." He smiled sadly. "Nine hours later, I stopped by Claire's apartment to see how things went and found her in the bathtub, her wrist sliced open." His voice trembled, emotion overwhelming him.

I squeezed my eyes shut, pushing down all the anger and pain that had plagued me since I received that phone call. I still couldn't believe it hadn't even been a week. It felt like so much longer. Like a lifetime had passed since I walked into that cold room and confirmed the lifeless woman lying on the metal table was my sister.

Clearing my throat, I looked at Ethan. "So you're telling me the last person who saw my sister alive was this bastard's...was Nick's ex-wife?"

"I'm not certain about that. All I do know is that Claire followed her and planned to talk to her about her suspicions. After that, I have no idea what she did or who she saw."

"Do you have a file that contains information on this Julia Prescott?" I asked, nodding toward the neatly stacked folders still sitting in front of him. He seemed to have a file on everyone else connected to this.

He sifted through them, finally finding the one he was looking for toward the bottom. "Here it is. Julia Prescott."

He opened it, flipping through dozens of pieces of paper. "Sent to foster care at the age of four, which was where Nick first became obsessed with her, since they were at the same foster home until she was adopted at the age of six.

"Through the years, Nick kept tabs on her. Even went so far as to enroll in the same college to get yet another master's while she worked toward a bachelor's, although she had no idea he was the same kid from the foster home. Drugged and raped her, which she had no knowledge of until about seven years ago when she found his stash of souvenirs and journals. He tried to prevent her from turning him in, but in a beautiful act of poetic justice…" A slow smile spread across his face, "she stabbed him in the balls."

I winced, despite knowing the guy deserved it. "Fuck…"

"Pretty epic, huh? The whole story's in here. Take a look for yourself."

He tossed the file onto the coffee table. When the folder fell open, revealing what appeared to be a victim photo taken by the police to document abuse, I sucked in a sharp breath, eyes widening.

It wasn't the bloody lips that shocked me.

Or the bruises on her cheekbones.

Or the swollen eye.

It was *who* was in that photo.

Her hair may have been a different shade, her eyes vacant and lackluster, but there was no mistaking the truth glaring back at me from those familiar, green orbs. Ones I'd recognize anywhere.

Belle was Julia Prescott.

Julia Prescott was Belle.

What.

The.

Fuck.

CHAPTER SIX

Julia

I gazed out the window of the town car as it drove away from the high-rise buildings that dotted the shoreline of Waikiki Beach after dropping Naomi off at her hotel. I would have been lying if I said I wasn't tempted to get a room myself. Pack up my stuff. Pretend I'd never accepted my brother's invitation to use one of his architecture company's rental properties on Oahu.

If I hadn't, if I'd kept to my original plan of staying in Waikiki, I never would have met Chris — Lachlan.

At this point, that would have been preferable to the inescapable truth that he'd used me.

I heard Naomi's voice in my head, scolding me that I didn't know that for certain. That perhaps there was another explanation.

I couldn't share in her optimism, though. I gave Nick the benefit of the doubt, and it nearly killed me.

All day, I'd barely been able to focus. I didn't know how I made it through the cooking segment or the handful of interviews I had. I just wanted to disappear, lock out the rest of the world, and forget I ever met Lachlan.

It should be easy enough. We'd only spent one night together.

One night that ended up being a lie. Simply a scheme to get information.

Nothing more.

I should have hated him for his deception.

A part of me did.

But another part wanted to separate the Lachlan who lied to me from the Chris who made me feel alive. And it was that part that had me entertaining the notion of simply pretending I'd never learned the truth. Keep using him for a week of hot sex. Give him nothing but my body in return.

But I wasn't that cunning.

That vindictive.

That sinister.

Not like it appeared Lachlan was.

I had really hoped turning forty would be the fresh start I needed. That I'd finally leave the horror of my thirties far behind.

I never expected them to follow me to paradise.

"We're here, ma'am," Paul, my driver, announced.

I snapped out of my thoughts, surprised the twenty-minute drive was already over, and peered up at the two-story beach house.

When I left earlier this morning, I was filled with so much hope, so much promise. Now, I feared I wouldn't be able to step one foot inside without being surrounded by Lachlan's betrayal.

After everything Nick put me through, I thought I knew enough not to trust so easily. Yet all it took was a panty-melting smile, a few kind words, and a touch that lit me on fire, and I was more than happy to lower my guard.

And my pants.

I couldn't put myself through that again.

I couldn't put *Imogene* through that again.

The car door opened. Paul helped me out before going to the trunk and retrieving my things.

"Do you need help bringing these inside?" he asked, pulling out my garment bag and makeup case, which more closely resembled a suitcase.

There was once a time when the only makeup I owned was some powder, blush, eyeliner, and a few tubes of lip gloss. Now I had everything under the sun, all to make me look the part my PR team had concocted in the hopes of differentiating the Julia Prescott who made cakes and pastries from the Julia Prescott whose husband was responsible for nearly a dozen rapes and murders.

"I can manage." I took the garment bag from him and draped it over my arm, then grabbed the handle of my makeup case.

"Nine o'clock tomorrow?"

"See you then." I forced a smile, inwardly cringing at the idea of enduring another day of pretending. Of putting on an act. Of being someone I wasn't.

Then I headed up the walkway and into the quiet house.

Feet screaming for relief, I stepped out of my heels and dropped my things in the entryway before proceeding into the kitchen. I stopped when my eyes fell on the humming-bird cake on the island, two slices missing.

My stomach clenched, an ache filling my heart at the memory of Lachlan. Of how understanding he was. How he cheerfully agreed to bake a cake with me, since baking was always my happy place. How, over the course of our time in the kitchen, all my nerves about having sex for the first time in seven years evaporated to the point that I felt comfortable enough to give him exactly what he wanted.

But none of it was real. It was all an act, a ruse.

I grabbed the bottle of red wine off the counter, poured a healthy amount into a nearby glass, and made my way toward the lanai, hoping some fresh air and good wine would give me the clarity about what I was going to say to Lachlan when I saw him.

If I should even bother.

Disappearing sounded more and more appealing with every second.

But as I opened the door, I came to an abrupt halt at the sight of the man sitting on the wicker couch, shoulders hunched, forearms resting on his knees. His expression was pained, turmoil covering every inch of him.

He didn't look like the same confident, debonair man who left me this morning.

He looked...shattered.

I had to fight the urge to go to him, wrap him in my arms, give him the comfort he so easily provided me last night. Hell, since our first meeting.

But I couldn't do that. *Refused* to do that. I'd learned my lesson with Nick. I vowed to never subject myself to any more mind games. Any more traps. And that was probably all this was. Simply a trap. One I wouldn't fall for again.

"What are you doing here?" I demanded, my voice hard.

He snapped his head up, eyes glassy and tinged with red. It appeared as if he'd been...crying? Or at least struggling to hold in his emotions. But why?

Then I noticed his phone on the coffee table in front of him. When I saw the photo on the screen, I wavered, my legs almost giving out beneath me as I swallowed the bile rising in my throat.

I'd hoped to never see that photo again, a near impossibility considering it was one all the news sites displayed when reporting on Nick's crimes. They always used a photo of Nick in his tweed jacket, tie, and dark-rimmed glasses, exuding the intellectual he was. But the one they used for me was snapped after I fought to finally free myself from his control. My face was pale, apart from the bruises on my cheek, eye, and jaw, my lips swollen and bloody, hair disheveled.

I wished I could erase that woman from my memory. Wished I could just move on from my past, instead of constantly be reminded of it, no matter how hard I tried.

I just wanted to be free.

I doubted I ever would be.

"Is this you?" Lachlan asked in a shaky voice, jaw tight, muscles strained.

Summoning all the strength I possessed, I held my head high when all I really wanted to do was curl into a ball and disappear at the memory that image evoked.

"I don't know—"

"*Answer me!*" he bellowed, shooting to his feet and advancing.

I instinctively backed up, fear snaking through me. The shock caused me to loosen my grip on the wine glass. It crashed to the ground, glass shattering, wine staining the pavement a dark red color, reminiscent of the blood that had stained the cement when I made my final stand against Nick.

Lachlan immediately stiffened, lips parting, regret pooling in his azure eyes as they skated over me in concern.

"Fuck. I'm sorry." He hung his head, scrubbing a hand over his face. "I just..." Pulling his lips between his teeth, he returned his gaze to mine. "I need to know." His chin quivered. "Is the woman in the photo you? Please," he begged.

I studied him for a beat. His anguish seemed...authentic. I wanted to believe it was real.

But experience had taught me to always be skeptical. To always second-guess anyone's motives, even if my gut told me he wasn't faking this. The emotion in his eyes was too raw. Too cutting. Too deep. I felt it in my bones.

"You obviously already know the answer," I shot back, averting my gaze. Partly because I couldn't bear to look into his pained eyes. Partly because I didn't want him to see the uncertainty in mine. "Why else would you have agreed to my proposition?"

He took a timid step toward me, brows scrunched. "What do you mean?"

"Oh, come off it." I threw my hands up in frustration. "You can stop with the act now, Chris." I glared at him, lip curling in the corner. "Or should I say *Lachlan?*"

He inhaled a sharp breath, eyes going wide.

"That's right. I know who you are, too."

He opened his mouth, but I continued before he could say anything.

"So you can stop pretending you just put the pieces together when it's obvious you've known all along. You're simply trying to cover your ass because you must have seen me on the *Morning Show* earlier today. When my segment aired right after they did a piece about you and your sister, you realized you needed to do damage control since the chances were high I'd seen it and figured it all out."

He looked at me quizzically. "Figured out what exactly?"

"Why you agreed to my proposal. Why you baked a fucking cake with me, for crying out loud. It wasn't just to get laid."

With every word I spoke, my resolve that he had to have known increased. It would be too much of a coincidence to think otherwise.

Eyes on fire, I leaned toward him. "You hoped by fucking me, I'd tell you what I refused to tell your sister." I placed my hands on my hips. "Well, I'm sorry to be the one to inform you, but I do not speak to my ex-husband. Why the hell would I?

"Since the truth about all that shit came out..." I gestured to his phone, "I've done everything I can to put it all behind me. To protect my daughter. The absolute last thing I would ever do is jeopardize her safety. So when your sister accosted me in public, *in front of my daughter*, I had no choice but to keep her as far away from us as possible."

I took a deep breath, calming myself. "So now, if you're done pretending to be blindsided about who I am, please see yourself off my property."

Ignoring the nagging voice in my head that sounded eerily like Naomi's, urging me to at least listen to what he had to say, I spun, my feet not carrying me nearly quickly enough toward the house and my escape.

It probably took only a few seconds to reach the sliding

glass door, but with the heat of Lachlan's intense stare scalding my skin, it felt like hours, each step I took away from him filling me with an increasing sensation of doubt.

Then a barely audible whisper cut over the sound of the crashing waves, the sincerity and raw vulnerability within giving me pause.

"You're wrong."

CHAPTER SEVEN

Julia

His voice was so low, yet it reverberated through me as if a powerful demand. I couldn't help but hesitate at the resignation. The sadness.

The hurt.

Based on what I knew to be true — a true crime podcaster confronting me about my ex-husband, then her brother, a professional baseball player who could sleep with any woman he wanted, agreeing to a one-week fling with me, a forty-year-old woman — I had no reason to believe him.

To *trust* him.

But Naomi's relentless voice echoed in my head, begging me to listen to him. To consider the idea that maybe our paths crossed because of a bigger reason. That we were, as she put it, "two lost souls who desperately needed to be found".

And that was exactly how I felt before I met Lachlan. Like I was lost, bobbing on an ocean under a starless night, looking for a compass to steer me home. Nothing in my life had ever made sense.

Until him.

I felt it the first time his skin brushed mine. This pull toward him.

And it was this pull that prevented me from walking away from him right now, a force bigger than me keeping me frozen in place.

I looked over my shoulder. "Wrong?"

He slowly nodded, taking several deliberate steps toward me. I fully faced him, pulse quickening at the intensity and determination in his gaze.

"Yes, Belle...Julia." His chest heaved, jaw tense. "You're wrong. I didn't accept your proposition to get information out of you. Hell, I didn't even know who you were until I learned Claire had a goddamn true crime podcast, something I had no idea about until a few hours ago."

"Then why—"

"I accepted your proposition because, from the moment I met you, I couldn't stop thinking about you. Because you're a beautiful woman who has this infuriating, yet charming ability to make me laugh. Something I haven't done much of in quite a few years, I'm afraid."

He closed the final few inches separating us, only leaving a sliver of space. I tried to ignore the electricity sizzling in the air, remind myself it wasn't real. That it was all a lie.

But I couldn't ignore the way he looked at me with so much anguish, as if he'd just learned an awful truth.

Maybe he had.

"And because I knew I'd regret it every day if I didn't do everything I could to spend as much time with you as you were willing to give me. Make no mistake. You're the absolute last thing I need in my life right now. Even more so now that I know who you are and everything that goddamn bastard..." He trailed off, voice catching.

Just a few days ago, this man was a mystery to me, rarely showing a hint of emotion.

Now he practically broke down at the knowledge of who I was and what Nick had put me through. I didn't know how to respond, what to think.

"I've dealt with a lot of crap in my life," he continued, voice heavy with heartache. His nostrils flared. Muscles strained. Veins in his neck throbbed.

Every inch of him radiated pain and sorrow to the point that I physically felt his grief. And it wasn't over losing his sister. It was because of what I'd silently endured for years, too petrified of what would happen to Imogene to voice my suspicions to anyone. A prisoner in a life Nick made for me.

In a way, I still was.

"But what I learned today..." He pulled his lip between his teeth. Then he cupped my face in his strong hands.

I inhaled a sharp breath at the initial contact, especially considering mere minutes ago, I wanted to get as far away from him as possible. But I couldn't resist him, craving his touch. His peace. His comfort. His understanding.

I melted into him, heart aching at the emotion emanating from his fingertips as he held me the way I'd always dreamed about being held.

There was no hint of deception. Of possessiveness. Of manipulation.

It was real. Pure. Honest.

"I've never wanted to hurt someone as badly as I did. As I still do." His eyes skated over my face, as if he were seeing me for the first time.

And that was precisely what this felt like. As if we were finally seeing each other for the first time. No more lies. No more charades. No more pretending. I was who I was. He was who he was. It was a gut-wrenching revelation, but also a freeing truth.

"I need to know you're okay. That you're safe. That the bastard can't hurt you. Because, I swear to God, if he—"

"I'm okay." I touched his face, placating him. "I'm safe. He can't get to me," I assured him, although I had my doubts.

I knew from experience that Nick's obsession with me knew no bounds. I didn't want to tell Lachlan that, though. Didn't want to worry him more than it appeared he already was. It wasn't worth it. Not when we'd only agreed to a week together.

Although I had a sneaking suspicion we'd moved far past that original agreement. That neither of us would truly be able to walk away after this revelation, our lives too intertwined to truly separate, even if all reason told us we needed to.

He closed his eyes, every muscle in his body relaxing. Then he rested his forehead on mine, exhaling a shaky breath. I breathed him in before releasing a breath of my own, the two of us not moving for several moments, simply enjoying this connection.

And through this connection, touching *alo* to *alo*, as he had said when he first told me about the *honi*, the traditional Hawaiian greeting, his truth was unmistakable. He didn't need to utter a single syllable. In this moment, I felt that deep, spiritual connection he claimed native islanders experienced when touching bone to bone and exchanging breaths. I felt his soul, his life, his heart.

His truth.

And I hoped he felt mine, too.

"So you really had no idea who I was," I commented. He gradually pulled away and met my eyes. My statement wasn't an accusation. More one of wonder, of disbelief.

He shook his head subtly. "I really had no idea who you were."

"I guess I *should* go ahead and buy that lottery ticket then, huh?"

He laughed, an endearing smile tugging on his lips. "You probably should."

It was silent for a beat before I asked, "What do we do now?"

"You mean after I pick up all this glass?" He nodded toward the broken wine glass a few feet away. Then he ran a hand through his dark hair, sighing deeply. "Your guess is as good as mine, but maybe going back to the beginning might be a good idea."

"The beginning?"

He stepped back and extended his hand. "I'm Lachlan Hale. In case you have absolutely no idea who I am, I'm a left-handed pitcher for Atlanta."

"So I've heard." I laughed slightly as I placed my hand in his. "Apparently your face is plastered all over the city, but I guess I never looked up long enough to notice."

Adjusting his hand to link our fingers, he took a small step toward me. "But that's *what* I am. Not who."

I nodded, knowing all too well what that was like. That had been my story most of my life.

First, I was the lucky little girl adopted by the Bradfords, one of Atlanta's most influential families. Then I was the wife of a psychotic serial killer. Recently, I was the woman behind one of the most popular bakery chains in the country.

"Then who are you, Lachlan Hale?" I asked softly, unsure I was ready to go down this road. We'd agreed in the beginning. No names. No sob stories. No expectations. All that seemed to be tossed out the window now that the proverbial curtain had been pulled back.

"Honestly, I'm still trying to figure that out. But I can tell you I love thunderstorms, the smell of a real Christmas tree, and a great bottle of red wine."

I fought to reel in my smile at the memory of the first bottle we'd shared. Neither of us thought anything would ever come of it. At least I didn't. I still struggled to wrap my head around the fact it had only been forty-eight hours since then. It seemed like so much longer. Like I'd known him for months instead of mere days. Like our souls had known each other most of our lives and our bodies were now just catching up.

Maybe they were.

His expression sobered. "And five years ago, I witnessed the girl I thought I'd spend the rest of my life with be brutally assaulted in our own home mere seconds before she drew her last breath."

"Lachlan...," I exhaled, heart squeezing at the thought of enduring something so traumatic.

No wonder he seemed so closed off when we first met. If I were in his shoes, I'd probably detest all of humanity myself.

"I'm so, so—"

Before I could finish, he dropped my hand and cupped my cheek. "But do you want to know the truth?"

"What's that?" I whimpered, the heat and intensity in

his gaze causing a shiver to roll through me, my stomach fluttering.

"You make it possible to breathe again."

He held my gaze, nothing but stark vulnerability and honest sincerity filling his brilliant, blue eyes.

Then he cleared his throat, dropping his hold on me and stepping back, increasing the space between us. "So there you have it. That's me. Take it or leave it."

I stared up at him as the ocean breeze wrapped around us. A part of me wanted to tell him this wasn't part of our original arrangement. That this wasn't supposed to happen. He was never supposed to know who I was. I was never supposed to know who he was. And we weren't supposed to share these tortured pieces of ourselves. The parts of our souls we tried to keep under lock and key.

But something about Lachlan made sense. Maybe because he'd suffered something horrific and traumatic. I may not have had to endure such gruesome violence and depravity like it sounded he did. But I knew what it felt like to lose your faith in humanity.

So instead of closing up, pushing him away like I normally would, I did the one thing I swore I never would again.

I gave this man my truth, in all its tragic ugliness.

"My name is Julia Prescott, which confuses everyone since I was adopted by the Bradfords, then married a professor. But instead of taking his last name, I kept my birth mother's. My favorite person in the world, besides my daughter and brother, was my meemaw. She taught me how to cook. Now I own a national chain of bakeries called The Mad Batter."

He closed his eyes as realization washed over him, a small chuckle escaping. "I knew you had to be some sort of pastry chef. I'll admit. I've cheated a time or two on my diet by getting some treats from your bakery in Buckhead."

I smiled. "I hope it was worth it."

"I will never regret anything when it comes to you." A peaceful smile lit up his expression, something in the way he peered at me telling me he was talking about more than just cheating on his diet.

When his stare became too meaningful, too penetrating, I averted my gaze. "I love the smell of burning leaves in the fall, the sound of cicadas in the summer, and there's nothing that makes a bad day good more than feeling my daughter's arms around me."

"That's really sweet."

"And when I was young and foolish, I made the horrible mistake of marrying a man just to gain the approval of my adoptive mother. A man who was calculating and manipulative. A man who, whenever I contemplated leaving him, did something to remind me who was in charge. Who held all the power. He'd threaten to take my daughter from me. Threatened to hurt all the people I loved. Something to put the fear in me. So, for the longest time, I stayed quiet, a prisoner in my own life. It wasn't until my brother started dating a girl we found out had been raped by Nick and decided to stand up for herself that I found the strength to do the same."

With every word I spoke, Lachlan's expression tightened, muscles tense, nostrils flared. His reaction shouldn't have surprised me, especially considering the state he was in when I saw him sitting on my lanai mere minutes ago. But the anger vibrating off him touched me. Made me feel like I wasn't alone.

"So there you have it," I said with a sad smile, mimicking his words. "That's me. Take it or leave it."

He studied me for several excruciating seconds. I'd never felt so exposed before. I shouldn't have been this nervous. He already knew who I was. But it didn't make it any easier as I waited for him to speak. To say *something*.

Just when I didn't think I could handle the silence a moment longer, he advanced, clutching my face as his lips descended toward mine. But he didn't kiss me. Not yet.

"It's nice to finally meet you, Julia," he murmured.

My heart warmed at the sound of my real name on his tongue, sexy Australian accent and all.

"And it's nice to finally meet you, Lachlan."

His lips curved into a smile as he started to erase the distance between us. But before he could, I pulled back, pressing a finger to his mouth.

"This still doesn't change anything," I told him, although my words lacked any conviction. "Our original agreement remains intact. At least the parts we didn't just obliterate." I laughed nervously, avoiding his intense gaze.

"We may now know who each other is. May have shared our truths."

I licked my lips, summoning the strength to get this out in the open. It shouldn't have been so difficult to reiterate the agreement we'd made.

Now, though, it felt...wrong.

"Regardless, I still need to walk away when this week is over. Especially given who you are. After everything my daughter went through when my ex was arrested and during his trial, the media constantly hounding her, scrutinizing everything she did, wondering if she would follow in her father's footsteps..." I shook my head. "I won't do anything that has the potential to bring attention to her. And this..." I gestured between our two bodies. "That's exactly what would happen.

"I may be jumping the gun," I continued, my words coming quickly, evidencing my nerves. "Hell, you probably think I'm crazy for even entertaining the notion you'd want whatever this is to continue. And perhaps I am. But I—"

"Agreed," he interjected. "One week. No expectations. No falling in love."

"No falling in love," I repeated as I swallowed past the ache in my throat.

I shouldn't have felt so much as a hint of sorrow over his promise, but the finality hit me harder than I expected. This was what I wanted. Needed.

Then why did it feel as if something inside me had died?

"Now that *that's* settled, can I finally kiss you as Julia?"

Smiling, I hoisted myself onto my toes, wrapping my arms around his neck. "I'd really like that."

When his mouth touched mine in a soft kiss, I exhaled, all the tension and unease leaving me. He brought both hands to my face, holding me close, our kiss tender and inviting at first. Then he deepened the exchange, coaxing my lips to part.

This wasn't the first time I was treated to one of his kisses. Hell, over the last twenty-four hours, I'd enjoyed more of them than I could possibly count.

But without the façade of pretending to be someone else, it felt like our first kiss all over again. It felt...real. The most real thing I'd experienced in quite a while.

Maybe ever.

Bringing the kiss to an end, he met my eyes. The power within made my stomach come alive with the fluttering of thousands of butterflies, making me feel like I was flying. And that was what being with Lachlan felt like. Like I was flying.

"I like kissing Julia," he confessed, thumb brushing along my bottom lip.

"And I like kissing Lachlan." I smiled before my expression fell.

He frowned, eyes tracing over my face in concern. "What's wrong?"

"I don't know. Perhaps I should rethink our agreement. I mean, I like kissing Lachlan." Flashing him a coy smile, I playfully batted my lashes. "But what if I don't like the way Lachlan does...other things?"

He looped an arm around my waist, yanking my body against his. When he circled his hips, his length pressing against my stomach, a rush of excitement shot through me.

Minutes ago, I was convinced he was only interested in me because I could give him the information his sister had been after.

But as I peered at the heat in his gaze, I had no doubt I couldn't have been more wrong about his motives.

This man wanted me.

And, my god, I wanted him in more ways than I thought possible after only knowing him a matter of days.

It should have petrified me.

But I wasn't going to allow it to. I was going to put myself first. Live in the moment until our story came to an end.

And it would end.

It had to.

"Trust me, beautiful," he crooned, wrapping his hand around my throat, making my gaze meet his, the possessiveness mixed with tenderness in his hold exactly what I craved. "I will endeavor to ensure that Lachlan pleases you just as much, if not more, than the man you were with last night. If you're agreeable, I'd like to start now. I think eight would do the trick."

"Eight?" I arched a brow, heart hammering at the lust

radiating off him as his intense stare traveled down my dress-clad body.

"Yes, Julia. If my calculations are correct, and they usually are, Chris gave you seven orgasms last night. It's only fair Lachlan surpasses that number. After all, I'm known for being rather competitive." He moved his hips, his arousal teasing me in the most scintillating of ways. "What do you say? Does that sound like something you'd be interested in?"

I nibbled on his bottom lip. "I have a feeling I'm *really* going to like Lachlan."

"I hope so, Julia. I *really* bloody hope so."

CHAPTER EIGHT

Julia

Before I had a chance to allow any lingering reservations I had about Lachlan to fester and turn into something more, his lips landed on mine, reminding me why I wanted this in the first place.

Why I wanted him.

With one kiss, he made me feel desired.

With one sweep of his tongue, he ignited something inside me I'd assumed never existed.

With one kind word, he made me want to drown in everything he was and never come up for air.

After everything I'd endured, didn't I deserve this?

Why was it so hard for me to let myself be happy?

Lachlan pulled back, his piercing, blue eyes meeting mine. "Don't."

I blinked, unsure how he could sense my unease.

Then again, that seemed to be a talent of his. Always able to pick up on my innermost thoughts and feelings without me uttering a single word.

Naomi's annoying voice sounded in my head again, insisting it was because we were connected on a deeper level.

Maybe she was right.

Maybe that was why I was currently doing everything to sabotage my happiness, especially when it came to Lachlan.

Because everything about this, everything about *him*, absolutely petrified me. Now that all our cards were on the table, I feared the only thing protecting me from falling for him had been eviscerated.

"I can practically hear the battle inside your head." He narrowed his gaze. "Trust me. I get it. This was never part of the plan. We weren't supposed to know anything about each other." He smoothed a tendril of hair behind my ear.

Everything about this man was contradictory, yet perfect. One minute, he was overcome with intense passion, his anger and anguish seeming to get the best of him. The next, he was gentle, tender.

"Since Piper died..." He swallowed hard, the pain from that loss obviously still affecting him, even if he wished it didn't. "Let's just say I've gotten really good at being someone I'm not. Thought it wouldn't hurt so much. And after everything you've been through, I get the feeling you've also gotten damn good at pretending to be someone you're not." He arched a brow. "Am I right?"

I nodded subtly, doing my best to keep my emotions in check. For years, I had no choice but to keep it all inside. First with my adoptive mother, then with Nick. Emotions were merely something to be used against me. A commodity to be bargained for, mostly to my detriment.

"Tonight, I don't want to be with the person you've pretended to be. And I'm not talking about just these past few days, but also for the last God knows how many years of your life."

My heart thrummed in my chest as I searched his eyes. I wanted to remind him this wasn't part of our agreement. That I'd insisted on keeping things light and meaningless for a reason.

But was that truly the case? Had this ever been just a meaningless fling? I doubted it. From the first time he rested his forehead on mine and we exchanged a breath, I felt more connected to him than I thought possible. Felt his pain, his heartache, his hope.

He cupped my cheek, his lips slowly inching toward mine. "And tonight, my beautiful Julia, I don't want you to be with the same man I've forced myself to be. I know I may be asking a lot of you...and myself. Hell, I'm not sure I even know how to stop pretending, how to be who I really am. If I even know who that is anymore. But right now, I think we owe it to ourselves to try. So that's what we're going to do, Julia. We're going to fucking try."

He crushed his mouth to mine, heat, passion, and pain coursing through my veins. I wrapped my arms around his neck, urging him closer, to kiss me harder as my need for him grew to a fever I didn't think possible. My head screamed to retreat, that this wasn't a good idea. That there was a reason I'd kept my walls up. Because the instant I lowered them, my guard would be down.

And that was when bad things happened. They always did.

But I was so tired of being that person. Of always pretending I was okay. Of having to keep everyone out so *he* couldn't use them to get to me.

For the first time in my life, I was with someone who wanted to be with me. The *real* me. And I was going to enjoy this all the way to the proverbial scene of the crash.

"Bedroom," I exhaled once he tore his lips from mine, his mouth trailing a torturous line down my jaw and to my neck.

"Eager much?" he teased as he nibbled on my earlobe.

"Just looking out for you," I said through my labored breaths, squeezing my thighs together. "You did promise me eight orgasms. It's probably best we get started now. Don't you think?"

His eyes locked with mine. "You know, I do think you're right."

"Good." I pushed away from him and turned, taking the few steps to the back door.

But before I could open it, he clutched my forearm and

spun me back around to face him. A gasp fell from me as he pinned me against the wall, his free hand skating down my body, lifting the hem of my dress.

"What are you—"

"Shh..." He hushed me with a kiss. "You said it yourself. I need to get to work on those eight orgasms I promised you. So I'm going to start by making you come with my fingers."

When he lifted my panties to the side and pushed my slickness around, thumb rubbing my clit, a moan fell from my throat.

"Then my mouth."

He peppered kisses along my collarbone as I moved against him, pleading with my body for the release I'd been craving all day. The release only he could give me.

"Then my cock."

He pushed a finger inside me, stretching and filling me. But it wasn't enough. This was simply a tease.

"Lachlan," I begged, breaths ragged as I sought that amazing bliss he treated me to repeatedly last night.

"Yes?"

"I need you inside me."

"And you have no idea how much I want to be inside you." He continued teasing me with his fingers, massaging and rubbing, pushing my body closer and closer to that edge I was only too happy to fall over with him. "But I want this more."

"Why? What can you possibly get out of fingering me?"

I closed my eyes, pulsing against him as I desperately chased my release.

Suddenly, he pulled away, increasing the space between us a fraction. It wasn't much, but with how badly I needed him, how tightly wound he'd left me, it might as well have been the length of a football field.

"What's—"

He looked at me curiously. "What do you mean by that?"

"Exactly what I said." I shrugged, avoiding his penetrating stare. "I mean, you're not getting much out of fingering me. I figured—"

"Stop."

The power in his voice cut me off, reverberating in the late afternoon air, the sky a cacophony of shades as the sun inched toward the horizon on the other side of the island.

"I just—"

"I'm not like him."

I didn't have to ask to whom he was referring. I knew.

"I don't use sex to control. To manipulate. I use it to find pleasure. Both mine *and* yours."

His lips gradually descended toward mine. "That's what I get out of fingering you," he whispered against my mouth as he grabbed my leg and hooked it around his waist. "Out of going down on you." His hand skated along my inner thigh before lifting my panties and resuming his ministrations, pushing a finger inside me, massaging and exploring. "I don't do it in the hopes you'll reciprocate."

He dropped his head to the crook of my neck, his unshaven jawline scraping, yet invigorating at the same time. I dug my hands into his hair, the combination of his words and motions heating my body into an inferno.

"I do it because I want to give *you* pleasure. Want to make *you* feel good." He pulsed against me, the thrilling sensation of his need pushing me to the brink, skin heating, breathing uneven. "Believe me when I say that seeing your face when you come, knowing I made you feel that good, well... I find *immense* pleasure in that."

"Oh god," I whimpered as his fingers hit that spot inside me I didn't even know existed twenty-four hours ago.

"That's right, baby. Don't fight it. I want you to come all over my fingers. Want to feel you clench around them."

His words were like a switch, setting me off as my orgasm ravaged through me. I tried to bite back my screams, considering we were outside. Anyone walking by or looking out their windows on either side of us would be able to see what we were doing.

But Lachlan had lit something inside me, making me no longer care what others thought. I wasn't going to view sex as something of which to be ashamed or embarrassed anymore. I was going to embrace it, enjoy it.

Because, my god, I definitely enjoyed being with this man.

"Holy fuck," I finally managed to say once my tremors died down.

Lachlan met my gaze, a smirk crawling across his

mouth. "There's one." He pressed his lips to mine in a soft kiss, then pulled back, keeping his hand on my hip as I attempted to straighten, my world still spinning around me.

Once he was certain I had my balance, he released me. Then, to my surprise, he reached for the hem of my skirt and proceeded to lift it once again.

"What are you doing?" I asked as he hooked his fingers into my panties, a salacious grin pulling on his mouth.

"What does it look like I'm doing?" He waggled his brows. "I'm taking off your panties."

"Shouldn't we head inside first?" I glanced past him, able to make out a few late-afternoon beachgoers.

"Don't tell me you're turning shy on me."

"I—"

"As tempting as the idea is, I'm not going to eat you out in front of an audience. In fact, I'm not going to eat you out right now at all. Or fuck you."

I furrowed my brows. "But I thought—"

"Don't worry. I promised you eight orgasms, and I never go back on my word." He pressed a kiss to my lips. "But I think we could both use some sustenance before resuming activities."

"Then why are you taking off my panties?"

He leaned toward me, breath warming my neck. "Because I want to watch you squirm, especially when I brush my hand up your leg so close to that delicious pussy." He pulled back. "And also because I want your panties."

"For what?" I asked, attempting to maintain my composure when I was seconds away from forcing him onto a nearby chair and crawling on top of him just to feel him between my legs.

"As a lucky charm."

"You're joking, right?

"Baseball players never joke about their lucky charms. These panties may just help our team make it all the way to the World Series." He winked.

"You're so twisted," I remarked with a laugh as I stepped out of my panties.

He shoved them into the pocket of his shorts, then looped an arm around me, tugging my body against his. "Oh, baby. If you want twisted, I will most definitely show you twisted."

CHAPTER NINE

Lachlan

The aroma of steak filled the kitchen as I scooped a little more butter on top of two gorgeous pieces of filet. Content with the sear on the outside, I slid on an oven mitt, then transferred the cast-iron pan into the hot oven to finish cooking.

A week ago if you had told me I'd be in Hawaii cooking dinner for a woman I just met, I would have laughed, then asked what you were on. But this... It felt right. Especially after the day Julia had. Before everything went to hell, I had planned to maybe take her to the leeward side of the island, show her the Mermaid Caves before grabbing something to eat.

But after everything we both learned, I figured a night in was a much better option. So I told her to take a bath while I ran to the market to pick up a few things for dinner. Truthfully, the idea of cooking for a chef was a bit nerve-racking, especially as I walked through the market, trying to figure out what to make when someone typically prepared most of my meals for me. I may not have gone to culinary school, but I knew I could make a decent steak.

"Now it's my turn for the fantasy."

That sweet, sultry voice cut through just as I snapped the ends off a few asparagus spears.

"What's that?" I glanced over my shoulder, my heart rate increasing as my eyes skated over Julia.

A floral sundress fell to just above her knees. Loose waves of auburn hair framed her face, which was now free from all the makeup she had on when she first arrived home. While I found her stunning no matter how she was dressed or the amount of makeup she wore, I preferred her natural beauty. Like now.

And what made her even more alluring was the fact she was comfortable around me just as she was. Because that was how I liked her. Just as she was.

"A man cooking dinner for me," Julia replied, sauntering toward me. She lifted herself onto her toes, her lips seeking mine.

I melted into her, savoring in the feel of her mouth on mine. And now that I knew the true woman, I treasured her kisses even more.

"Keep it up, and I'm likely to put that apron and heels back on," she murmured.

"Promise? Because if you're offering that in exchange for my relatively mediocre cooking abilities, I'm making you dinner the rest of the week."

She threw her head back, her laughter filling the space. Less than an hour ago, I didn't think I'd ever hear that beautiful sound again. Now I relished in it.

"Just so I'd wear that apron and heels again?" She brought her gaze to mine, lips pinched. "Need I remind you, you have an open invitation to see me naked anytime you'd like."

"And I plan on taking full advantage of that invitation." I flashed her a devious smile before my expression turned serious. I cupped her face, her skin so smooth compared to the roughness of mine. "But it's not about seeing you naked. That's not what I love so much about you in the apron and heels."

She frowned. "It's not?"

"No." I slowly lowered my lips toward hers, keeping her face locked in place so she couldn't escape. "It's about seeing you confident, Julia."

"Oh." She blinked, my words seeming to hit her harder than she anticipated.

I circled an arm around her waist and pulled her petite body against mine. She was so small compared to me. Another reminder we were as opposite as two people could possibly be. We made no sense as a couple. But in our bubble, we didn't have to make sense. And despite knowing the truth about each other, we were still in our bubble, hoping nothing would burst it.

At least until the end of the week when we'd pop it ourselves.

"That's why I found the apron and heels so damn sexy. Because of how bloody confident you were." I brushed my lips against hers, a tease of a kiss.

When she moaned, I couldn't resist the temptation, deepening the exchange, my hand roaming her frame. My tongue swept against hers as I lifted the skirt of her dress and squeezed her ass, causing her to yelp.

"Good girl," I commented slyly.

"What?" She pulled back, meeting my heated stare. "Sizing up my ass now?"

"Just making sure you didn't put any panties back on." I winked.

"I'd be a fool to do that." She pushed away and walked to the counter, grabbing a fresh bottle of wine and two glasses. "It would ruin my other fantasy."

"And what's that?"

She averted her gaze, a blush blooming on her cheeks.

"Don't get all shy on me now." I advanced, taking the corkscrew from her and tilting her chin up to meet my eyes. "What's your fantasy? How can I make it come true if I don't know what it is?"

She chewed on her lower lip for a moment, then drew in a breath. "Well, I had this image of enjoying a nice dinner with you. Easy conversation, as is always the case."

"And?"

Her pupils dilated, chest rising and falling in a quicker pattern. Then her voice dropped lower, more throaty. More husky. More...seductive.

"You'd be flirtatious, as you always are. But in this intoxicatingly sensual way." She edged toward me.

My muscles tensed, jaw clenching. Everything about this was such a damn turn-on. And what made my need for Julia even stronger was that she wasn't even trying to be sexy. This was just who she was.

"At some point," she continued, "the sexual tension between us would be too much."

I gripped her hip, lust coursing through me. "What would happen then?" I growled.

She smirked. "Be a good boy, and maybe you'll find out." She lifted herself onto her toes, her breath warming my neck. "But it involves you. A table. And me as dessert."

"Goddamn," I hissed, wrapping my hand in her hair as I crushed my lips to hers, claiming her mouth. I circled my hips, desperate for some sort of release of the hunger that had been building since she walked downstairs. Hell, since I fingered her on the lanai and took her panties.

"What I wouldn't give to have a taste of you right now," I grunted, burying my head in her neck as I nipped her skin. Then I pulled back. "But there's a special place in hell for people who overcook a steak. I guess we'll just have to delay our gratification."

Smiling slyly, she palmed my crotch. I inhaled a sharp breath.

"I guess we will," she murmured.

With a groan, I reluctantly stepped away from her, although the thought of foregoing dinner certainly seemed appealing.

"What do you need me to do?" Julia asked as I opened the oven, retrieving the sizzling cast-iron pan and placing it on a trivet. "Anything?"

"Actually, yes." I removed the oven mitt, tossing it onto the counter. "Come with me." I rested my hand on her lower back, leading her out onto the lanai.

A gentle breeze blew, the sky a beautiful pinkish orange as day gradually gave way to night. Soft music sounded from the speakers, the candles I arranged on the table completing the atmosphere.

"I want you to sit here and relax while I take care of you." I walked her toward the table, pulling out a chair.

"I don't mind helping," she protested, but I placed a gentle hand on her shoulder, forcing her to sit.

"From what I gathered, you've spent your whole life putting everyone else's needs before your own. So, for the next week, my goal is to take care of you the way you deserve. To ensure you put yourself first for once."

She tilted her head back, staring at me in awe. This was the least I could do for her. Literally. It was something so small. Yet to her, it was everything. The perfect gift.

"Thank you."

"Of course."

I leaned down, brushing a kiss against her cheek. Then I hurried back inside to finish preparing dinner.

I couldn't help but marvel at the entire scenario, and not simply because the last person I cooked for was Piper and I didn't think I'd ever find someone I wanted to cook for again.

After I learned who Julia was, I debated walking away. It seemed like the rational thing to do. Hell, it still did.

But after Ethan returned to his hotel and I went for a walk to clear my head, I somehow ended up here, just as I did yesterday afternoon when I overheard Julia's proposition.

And just like yesterday, it was as if the universe was giving me a sign, telling me this was where I needed to be.

That this was what I needed in my life.

I just prayed this decision wouldn't come back to haunt me.

CHAPTER TEN

Lachlan

"Well, color me impressed, Lachlan Hale." Julia dabbed her mouth with her napkin. "Amazing in the bedroom *and* the kitchen." She smirked, meeting my gaze from across the table. "What more could a girl ask for?"

I shrugged dismissively. "It's just steak."

"There's no such thing as 'just steak'. Steak is a complex cut of meat that needs to be properly understood in order to be prepared correctly. So many people soak it in marinade, then char the fuck out of it. But you... You knew all you really needed to bring out its natural flavor was salt and pepper."

"And butter," I reminded her. "Don't forget the butter."

"That's a given. Butter makes everything better."

"Agreed." I lifted my glass, warmth filling me as I admired her.

Throughout the course of our meal, we enjoyed the same easy conversation as always. But tonight, it felt even easier. There was no longer this invisible line drawn about what we could and couldn't discuss. We were finally free from the chains we'd shackled around ourselves. It was liberating in a way I hadn't expected.

"Although, I will confess, it took a lot of trial and error to figure it all out," I added after taking a sip of wine. "There was a time not so long ago when the only thing I could cook was Ramen noodles. Or boxed macaroni and cheese. Granted, when I played minor league ball, that was pretty much all I could afford."

"They don't pay well?"

I barked out a laugh. "Not even close. I probably would have made more working at a grocery store."

Most people had no idea what it was like in the minors. It wasn't the glamorous life that often went along with being in the major leagues. Hell, most of my teammates had to work second, even third jobs just to make ends meet. Then there was the cramped housing, sometimes six or eight of us in a small apartment. Life in the minors tested you, made you question whether it was worth it. For many, it wasn't.

For me, though, it was worth the sacrifice. I knew I wouldn't be happy until I gave it my all. And that meant putting up with the low pay and overcrowded living conditions.

"The minors is kind of like military training for baseball players. Weed out those who aren't ready to put in the hard work. A lot of guys can't handle it."

"How long were you in the minors?"

"About four years. I was recruited my senior year in high school. It was either go to UCLA and play ball there or head straight to the minors. It wasn't as easy a decision as you might think," I added quickly. "There was a lot to consider. Some players go to college, play ball there, get a degree, then are recruited straight to the majors. In the end, Claire was the one who encouraged me to follow my dream. She may be a year younger, but she's always been my voice of reason." I smiled nostalgically as I peered into the distance. "Or she was."

Julia placed her hand over mine. "I'm sorry."

I brought my eyes back to hers, offering her a small smile. "Thank you."

I held her gaze for a beat, then pulled away, clearing my throat. "You mentioned you have a brother. Are you two close?"

She beamed, the affection she held for him obvious. "He's my best friend. Granted, we may not always see eye to eye on certain things, and we certainly get into our fair share of disagreements, but at the end of the day, we know we love each other, even if we may not *like* each other at that precise moment."

I swallowed hard, her words bringing to mind my relationship with Claire.

Ever since her death, I'd buried myself in guilt, angry at the world and myself for taking her for granted. If there was anyone who knew how fleeting life could be, it was me. Regardless of the distance I put between us in her final months, I hoped she knew how much I cared for her. How much I appreciated her.

How much I loved her.

"The last time I spoke to Claire, we had an argument," I confessed.

I wasn't sure what compelled me to do so. What I was searching for. Forgiveness. Redemption. Absolution.

Julia straightened. "About what?"

I opened my mouth, hesitating.

"You don't have to tell me," she added quickly. "It's none of my business. It's not part of our arrangement anyway."

"Our arrangement...," I mused, laughing to myself.

Bringing the glass of wine to my lips, I took a sip, savoring in the robust Syrah that was the perfect complement to the steak. Then I set it back down, focusing on Julia, her eyes shining as a gentle breeze blew around us.

"When I first overheard your proposal, I thought it was the perfect way to escape being me for a minute. Everywhere I go, people know who I am. Don't get me wrong. Since I was a little boy, I had dreams of playing professional baseball. I wanted that fame and notoriety. Wanted to have my face on billboards and merchandise. Wanted to have fans scream my name as I stepped onto the field." I licked my lips. "But there's so much about living in the spotlight they don't tell you. That nothing can possibly prepare you for."

"I get it." She offered me a sympathetic smile. "I mean, I can't entirely understand what it's like, since our situations are vastly different. But I can tell you I wasn't prepared for my name and face to be plastered all over newspapers and on television screens after..." She trailed off, searching for the words. "Well... After everything that transpired."

I reached across the table. Clutching her hand in mine, I attempted to offer her some sort of comfort, reminding her that part of her life was behind her. And if I had anything to say about it, that was where it would remain.

"But something about you," I continued, running my thumb along her knuckles, "makes me want to talk about these things. Maybe it's because you've been through some serious shite yourself. I don't know. All I do know is that from the beginning, from the minute I first laid eyes on you... You make it not hurt so much, Julia."

She parted her lips as my confession hung in the air between us. Then she smiled. "You make it not hurt so much, too, Lachlan."

I stared deep into her emerald eyes, so many emotions swirling within. Now that we'd lowered our defenses, she had no problem allowing me to see the pieces of herself she'd locked away, probably for years. Did she see the same when she looked at me?

The thought should have petrified me.

But it didn't.

"Claire wanted to talk to me about Piper. About the night she died," I said, pulling my hands from her. "That's what caused our argument."

"Piper's your former girlfriend, correct?"

It didn't escape my notice that she referred to her as my former girlfriend, not my ex. Calling her my ex insinuated some sort of conscious decision to end things. Some sort of closure.

I never got that.

Never got to say goodbye.

"Claire didn't think Caleb, the guy they arrested, was responsible. She claimed the attacker was still out there, which I didn't want to believe. So I got angry. Told her nothing good would come out of bringing up that night. But now..." I blew out a breath. "I'm pretty sure she was right. That this guy *is* still out there. That's why she wanted to talk to you. See if her theory panned out."

"What theory is that?"

I leaned toward her, confusion crossing my brow. "She didn't tell you?"

"She tried to talk to me about Nick. About him potentially being connected to a bunch of recent crimes..." Her voice trailed off as she looked past me. I could practically see the puzzle pieces snap into place. Then she whipped her wide eyes back to mine. "She thought Piper's death had something to do with Nick?"

I nodded.

"But how? You said Piper died five years ago. Nick was in prison at that time."

"She didn't say unequivocally that Nick was responsible. Just that he was somehow *connected*."

"How?"

"The date. July tenth. That was the date Piper died five years ago. It was also the same date one of your husband's victims took her own life five years prior. A woman named Evelyn Price, a social media influencer. Just like Piper. This similarity struck Claire as odd, so she started looking into suicides. She found a pattern. A woman with the same profession as one of your ex-husband's victims was found dead of an apparent suicide on the same date."

Her jaw dropped as she processed this. Apparently, Claire hadn't gone into this much detail with her. I wondered what else Claire hadn't shared with her.

"But Piper didn't commit suicide, right?"

"You're right. She didn't. It was a home invasion. I made the same argument to Ethan when he told me Claire's theory."

"Who's Ethan?"

"He helped my sister with research for her podcast. Paid me an unexpected visit this afternoon to share what he knew. Made me stop and think about what could have happened if I weren't there. Ethan seemed to think that was why this guy didn't leave when he realized I was home. Why he knocked me out to the point it was a miracle I survived. Same with Claire, who'd stopped by unexpectedly and was stabbed in the stomach. He *had* to kill a social media influencer on July tenth and make it look like a suicide. It was a ritual. An obsession. He could have easily killed Claire and me, yet didn't. We weren't part of his ritual."

"Why didn't she go to the police with this?"

"She did, but they said any connection was tenuous, at best. That they couldn't build a case around mere coincidence. She needed something more concrete, which was why she was desperate to talk to you." I sighed. "Ask you about the jewelry."

A gasp fell from Julia's mouth, eyes flinging wide, every muscle in her body stiffening.

"J-jewelry?" she quivered. "What jewelry?"

"The jewelry," I answered cautiously, my pulse increasing. "Claire didn't ask you about that?"

"No." She slowly shook her head. "Once she started asking questions about Nick, I had her removed, not wanting Imogene to have to suffer through any more trauma." She blinked, worry lines forming around her eyes. "What jewelry is she talking about?"

"Claire's theory was that this guy is repeating Nick's kill cycle. Obsessively so. And because your ex-husband stole trophies and gave them to you as a gift..."

"Oh, my god..." She covered her mouth, her entire body trembling.

"What is it?" I asked frantically. Partly to make sure she was okay. Partly because I was desperate for answers about Claire.

And I had a feeling Julia held the key.

When she didn't immediately say anything, I leaned forward, gaze pleading. "Please, Julia."

"They told me it was nothing. Just some true crime fanatic obsessed with my husband's case. In my gut, I always knew it was more."

"What was?"

"Since the case made headlines, I occasionally received strange gifts. The FBI claimed it was harmless. Just fanatics doing what they do. And I never questioned their assessment." She lifted her gaze to mine. "Except..."

"Yes?"

"The past several years, I've received the periodic package with the return address of my corporate headquarters, making it impossible to trace the source. And they were always sent to one of my bakeries in the same packaging we use for official communications, ensuring someone would open it."

"And the contents of these packages?" I asked, even though I didn't need to. The answer was written all over her face.

"Jewelry."

CHAPTER ELEVEN

Julia

My eyes fixated on a chip in the wood of the wet bar as I sat on the couch, listening to Lachlan and Ethan tell Nikko, Lachlan's cousin and best friend, everything he'd shared with me.

Hell, even *more* than he'd shared with me.

This wasn't how I imagined meeting Lachlan's family. Not that I'd actually expected to meet them to begin with. It was never supposed to be part of the deal. I wasn't supposed to know anything about him.

But that was before.

Before I learned who he was.

Before I realized how intertwined our lives were.

Before the truth slammed into me, stealing every bit of oxygen from my lungs.

It wasn't over. Nick's influence still pervaded every part of my life, chaining me to him.

I was foolish to think I'd ever be free. He'd warned me I never would.

He was right.

"And you claim you received the first suspicious package approximately five-and-a-half years ago?" somebody asked, but the voice sounded distant. Like a question being asked on a police procedural we were watching. Like it wasn't real.

God, how I wished this weren't real.

"Ms. Prescott?" the voice pressed again when I didn't respond.

"Hey." A hand landed on my thigh, comforting and soothing. I snapped my head to my right, meeting Lachlan's concerned gaze. "Are you okay?"

I didn't know how to answer that. Was I okay? Had I ever been okay? I doubted it. So I did what I'd done my entire life.

"Sorry." I shook off the emotions trying to leak through the cracks in the wall I'd erected years ago. Straightening my spine, I plastered on a smile. "I'm fine. Just lost in my thoughts for a second."

"You don't have to pretend, Julia," Lachlan said in a low voice. "Not with me. If you're not okay, just say it and we'll stop. I know how difficult bringing up all this has been for me. I can't even begin to fathom what it's like for you."

"All the more reason we need to figure this out." I

squared my shoulders and looked at Nikko, his imposing stature dwarfing the tiny chair where he currently sat. And I thought Lachlan was a big guy. He was small compared to Nikko. "What was your question again?"

He stole a glance at Lachlan, as if asking if it was okay to proceed. I wasn't sure what Nikko saw in his gaze, but he eventually looked back at me, cautiously continuing.

"The first suspicious package...," Nikko began, his soothing voice at odds with his commanding presence. "When did you receive it?"

"Five years ago this past March."

"Autumn Quinn," Ethan announced, pushing the rolled-up sleeves of his button-down shirt up his forearms. He leaned toward the coffee table, grabbing a stack of files containing what I now knew to be all the research he and Claire had done. Not only on my husband and his victims, but all the recent suicides they believed to be the work of a copycat.

Or "acolyte", as I'd overheard Ethan refer to him.

I would have rather this guy simply be a copycat. Acolyte indicated some sort of cult-like follower.

Meaning this could still very well have been Nick's doing. That Nick was the one giving the orders.

A shiver rippled up my spine at the thought.

Finally finding what he was looking for, Ethan placed a photo of a woman onto the coffee table for every to see. She was just like every other woman in his files.

Young.

Beautiful.

Dead.

But there was something else that seemed familiar.

Or maybe I just saw pieces of myself in all the victims. A once vivacious woman whose life was ruined the instant they met Nick. Or whomever was doing this.

"A student at Emory. Volunteered with Homes for the Homeless."

I inhaled a sharp gasp, heat washing over me as I snatched the photo, scrutinizing it.

"What is it?" Nikko pressed.

"Homes for the Homeless…" I tried to pull a memory to the surface, but none would come. "That's my brother's charity."

"And your brother is?"

"Weston Bradford."

Nikko jotted something down in his notebook. Then he looked back at me.

"How can I reach him?"

"He lives in Atlanta. He—" I stopped short at the mounting curiosity and suspicion radiating off him. "Wait. You don't think *he's* responsible, do you?" I tossed the photo back onto the coffee table.

"I'm not sure *what* to think right now. In my mind, everyone's a potential suspect. Especially someone with ties to your husband."

"*Ex*-husband," I corrected.

"I apologize. Someone with ties to your *ex*-husband."

"I'll give you his number, but it's a waste of time. There's no way Wes is even remotely involved."

"She's right," Ethan added, coming to my defense.

Nikko cocked his head. "Care to elaborate?"

Ethan grabbed his pile of files and flipped through them once more. Then he threw a photo of a familiar woman onto the table.

"Because of her. Londyn Bennett. Now Bradford. Weston's wife. Before Nick graduated to being a serial killer and was simply a stalker and rapist, Ms. Bennett was one of his earlier victims. Tried to attack her again when they crossed paths about seven years ago, at which time Ms. Bennett defended herself by shooting him. But since her skin isn't exactly white, the cops arrested her. She nearly went to prison while Nick remained free." Ethan turned his attention to me. "Until Ms. Prescott discovered Nick's...*souvenirs*."

"I appreciate the information," Nikko said. "But that still doesn't—"

"Trust me," I insisted. "Wes was the only one who ever questioned me about Nick. Who was ever suspicious of him. Everyone else saw a charismatic pillar of the community. Plus, if Wes were somehow involved, he wouldn't be trying to convince me all these gifts I've received are more than just due to a true crime fanatic, as the FBI agent I've been in contact with said appeared to be the case, considering the absence of any evidence to the contrary. At least until now."

"What's the name of your FBI contact?" Nikko brought his pen back to his notepad.

"Agent John Curran. Out of the Atlanta office."

"I'll reach out to him. See what light he can shine on this. This doesn't mean Claire's theory is right. These gifts you received *could* simply be from a true crime fanatic. It's public knowledge that giving you a piece of the victim's jewelry was part of your ex-husband's signature. All these packages were sent to your bakeries, not your home. It truly could be anyone."

"But it *is* suspicious," Lachlan interjected. "Don't you think, cousin?"

Nikko blew out a breath. "I won't deny that. But until we can unequivocally connect each piece of jewelry to each one of these women, it's merely circumstantial. In order to prove or disprove, we'd have to reach out to the family members of twenty victims, according to Claire's research. The FBI will have to coordinate with local authorities. There's a lot of bureaucratic red tape that slows things like this down, especially if some outside law enforcement agency comes in and tries to convince the local PD that they got it wrong. That a death they ruled a suicide might actually be a homicide."

"Then we have to cut through the red tape," I insisted.

"And how do you propose we do that? There are procedures for a reason. We—"

"I understand that. But maybe there's a way to ascertain if we're on the right path or not. If Claire's theory holds any merit at all."

Nikko furrowed his brows. "What do you mean?"

I swallowed hard and turned to Lachlan. "Yesterday evening, my brother called. Told me about another gift. Another piece of jewelry delivered to one of my bakeries. If this theory is correct, the necklace I received could belong to the July tenth victim, who also happened to be a social media influencer."

"Claire...," he exhaled on a quiver, squeezing his eyes shut. "I never even thought... I don't know what I thought."

"Claire *was* an influencer," Ethan offered. "Or at least her alter ego was."

I grabbed my phone and opened my photos. When this all began, something compelled me to keep a record of each piece of jewelry I'd received. Maybe because I knew something was wrong. I just didn't know what.

And with each gift, I grew more and more uneasy.

My biggest fear was that Nick had a guy on the inside who sent the gifts to taunt me.

To remind me of the promise he'd made as he was taken away in handcuffs.

To warn me that I'd never be free from him until he drew his final breath.

Or I drew mine.

"Do you..." Lachlan didn't need to ask his question. I knew what it was.

I simply nodded as I stared into his eyes, not showing him my phone. Not until I knew he was ready.

After several long moments, he held out his hand. I placed my cell into it.

"Does that look familiar?" I asked softly, hopeful, yet also praying he didn't recognize the necklace.

Tense silence filled the room as Lachlan studied the photo Wes had texted me, the only sound that of the ticking of the clock and a faucet dripping somewhere in the house. Then he squeezed his eyes shut, his expression anguished.

"It was our mum's," he choked out, his voice heavy with a combination of heartache and anger. He returned his gaze to mine, eyes glossy from pent-up emotion. "Triple Koru. Represents the Circle of Life. After she passed, Claire wore it all the time. Said it made her feel close to our mum."

No one said anything, all of us staring at each other, not knowing how to proceed now that we had confirmation Claire's theory bore merit. It was almost easier when it was only a theory. Now it was real. There was someone out there emulating my ex-husband's kills. For what purpose? Was he involved?

God, I prayed he wasn't.

"How about July five years ago?" Lachlan asked after a beat. I tore my gaze to his as he wiped at his eyes. "Do you have a photo of what you received then?" His tone was determined, yet distraught.

I nodded subtly and took the phone back, scrolling through the photo album. When I found one dated July tenth five years ago, I stopped, admiring the gorgeous necklace — a simple, silver chain with a blue, heart-shaped charm made to look like an ocean wave. It was certainly unique, not something you'd find at your local jewelers. Based on the little information Lachlan shared about Piper, I was all but certain this once belonged to her.

I glanced around the room, both Nikko's and Lachlan's stare trained on me, hopeful, yet scared at the same time. This had the potential to rip open any old wounds that had healed.

And could also solidify Claire's theory.

Drawing in a deep breath, I held out my phone so they both could see. Nikko's grip on the arms of the chair tightened, nostrils flaring, body shaking as he struggled to rein in his anger. I was surprised the chair didn't shatter under the strength of his grip.

I looked at Lachlan, expecting to see the same rage and resentment. Instead, his head hung in resignation.

"I gave it to her after she won her first big surfing competition," he explained softly. "Had it specially made from a rock I found out on The Mokes that reminded me of an ocean wave. So that's what I had it turned into." He looked up, meeting my gaze, tear trickling down his cheek. "It was the one thing I searched for after that night. The one thing I wanted to hold onto. I thought it was gone forever."

We all remained silent for several long moments,

almost out of respect for Claire, for Piper, for all the women who'd lost their lives too soon.

Finally, Lachlan cleared his throat, angrily swiping at his eyes. "I think this is more than just coincidence now. Don't you?" He arched a brow in Nikko's direction.

"I do." His deep voice trembled as he attempted to come to terms with the truth that the person who took his sister from him was still out there. Still killing innocent women.

"So what do we do? How do we find this bastard?" Lachlan's question came out hard and rash.

"*We* don't do anything." Nikko gestured between their two bodies. "I know you want to get to the bottom of this... for more than one reason." He glanced my way before looking back at his friend. "But we're looking at a potential serial killer who's crossed dozens of jurisdictional lines to commit his crimes. This is..." He pushed out a breath, shaking his head. "This is far above my pay grade."

He looked at me. "This FBI contact of yours... Agent Curran... How familiar is he with your ex-husband's case?"

"He knows it inside and out. His niece was Annabelle Landry, Nick's first murder victim. Like Wes, he'd been suspicious of Nick long before the truth came out. Saw him for the monster he was. Before he got involved, the police had no idea the extent of his crimes. We thought Nick had only been stalking and raping women, which is bad enough. Agent Curran put the pieces together and tied him to the suicides of his victims."

Nikko looked up after jotting down everything I'd just relayed to him. "Then we start there. We've got three months."

"Three months?" Lachlan gave him a quizzical look.

"Until he strikes again," Ethan interjected, tossing a folder onto the table, *October Thirteenth* written in big, bold letters. "Although chances are he's already on the hunt."

CHAPTER TWELVE

Lachlan

I hung back as Nikko and Ethan said their goodbyes to Julia, both giving her comforting hugs, as if they were old friends. Not the relative strangers they were. That was what tragedy did to people. Brought them together. Gave them something in common to fight for.

"Walk me out, bruh?" Nikko looked my way.

I knew precisely what he wanted to discuss. It was the last conversation I wanted to have, especially after tonight. But Nikko wasn't going to let me avoid having it forever.

So, instead of wrapping Julia in my arms and trying to pretend my world hadn't been rocked to its core, I made my way toward him, kissing Julia on the temple and promising to be back soon. Then I followed Nikko out of the house.

At nearly ten at night, the quaint, beach community was peaceful. I had difficulty wrapping my head around just how much had transpired over the last few hours. From Ethan's surprise appearance. To learning what Claire had been looking into. To finding out who Julia was. To the truth that she may be the key to uncovering the identity of a serial killer.

From the moment I met Julia, I couldn't shake the feeling she was different. That our paths crossing wasn't simply a happy coincidence.

I never expected one jellyfish sting could have led to this.

"What's up, cousin?" I asked once we reached Nikko's truck and he turned to face me.

He briefly glanced over my shoulder at the house before returning his attention to me, his voice no louder than a whisper. "What's going on?"

"What do you mean?"

"Between you and Julia." He crossed his arms in front of his chest, his biceps stretching the traditional tattoos covering his arms. "What's the deal?"

"You were the one who practically pushed me to talk to her the other night." I shrugged. "So I did. When I learned who she was, I was just as surprised as you are. Probably more so."

"I understand all that, but what's the deal with you two?" He stepped toward me, seeming to choose his next words carefully. "It was one thing when she was just some *ha'ole* from the mainland here for a good time. But this—"

"She's not just some *ha'ole*," I gritted out through a clenched jaw.

He raised a brow. "Really?"

"I..." I shook my head, unable to explain my reaction.

I couldn't quite understand it myself.

"Do you have feelings for her?"

"It's not like that," I replied dismissively. "We made an agreement before either one of us knew who the other was. One week. No expectations. Then we walk away."

"And now?"

I shoved my hands into the pockets of my shorts. "Nothing's changed."

"Nothing's changed?" he hissed out in disbelief. "From where I'm standing, it seems *everything's* changed."

"No, it hasn't. I—"

"Listen, bruh." He placed his hands on my shoulders. "I'm happy for you. I've been trying to get you to meet a girl for years now."

"I've been with plenty of girls," I reminded him. A twinge of guilt settled in my stomach over the notion of talking to Piper's older brother about another woman.

When I first started hooking up again after her death, I did everything I could to hide them from him. The last thing I wanted was to lose him as a friend. As *ohana*. But he eventually called me out, claimed he wanted me to move on. That it wasn't healthy for me to continue to hold onto a ghost.

"You were never really *with* them," he argued. "Not emotionally. Since losing Piper, you've kept everyone at arm's length... Until now."

I rolled my eyes, stepping away from him. "What are you going on about?"

"You know exactly what I'm going on about," he mimicked. "I saw the way you looked at Julia. It wasn't the look of someone who's not interested. Hell, I don't even think I ever saw you look at Piper that way."

"We're just having some fun. She made it perfectly clear from the beginning that nothing could ever come of this. Now that I know who she is, I am in complete agreement."

"And if it could?"

"It *won't*."

He laughed under his breath. "So you're going to spend the week together and then... What? Walk away in the hopes of never seeing each other again? Hate to break it to you, but with all this shit going on, I don't exactly see how that's even remotely realistic.

"If this theory pans out, and it looks like that's a damn good probability, you're both involved, like it or not. Her ex-husband inspired the person who attacked Piper. Who took Claire from you. Hell, her ex could still be somehow involved."

"I know that, all right? That's been in the forefront of my mind all night. I can't *not* think about it. But, like I said, it doesn't matter. We agreed. One week. Nothing more. No matter what. Nothing more," I repeated for emphasis, unsure if it were for his benefit or mine.

Nikko studied me for a beat, his analytical gaze seeming to comb through every inch of me, as if looking for a clue. Some piece of evidence that would crack the case wide open. But I wasn't a case to be solved.

At least I didn't think I was.

A smug expression slowly formed on his face. "Are you sure about that? Are you sure that's really what you want?"

"I—"

"I know you." He leaned toward me. "Knew who you were before Piper died. Know who you've been since then. Since you turned into this closed-off ass who's done everything in his power to put up walls. To keep people out. Including your own family. Your own *ohana.*"

I opened my mouth to argue, but Nikko held up a hand. He knew I didn't have a leg to stand on in my defense. Worse, I did, too.

"But tonight, I saw a glimpse of the Lachlan I used to know before anger consumed him. Before guilt controlled him. And I get the feeling it's because of that woman in there." He pointed to the house. "I'm happy to see the man I used to know. The Lachlan who smiled more. Laughed more. And, dare I say it, loved more."

I whipped my gaze to his, eyes wide and panicked. "What are you suggesting?"

"I'm not suggesting anything. But I know what I saw. This isn't a passing fling. There are feelings involved. Hers *and* yours."

"That doesn't matter," I insisted yet again, although my words became increasingly unconvincing with each breath. "That's not our deal."

"Maybe not right now. But what if she changes her mind about your arrangement? What if she tells you she doesn't want to walk away?"

I vehemently shook my head, heart squeezing. I wasn't sure if it were over the idea of her changing her mind and me hurting her, or her *not* changing her mind and her hurting me.

"You were in there. You know who she is. Who her ex-husband is. That fucker still petrifies her. Has her watching her every move. Has her held captive. Even from behind prison walls, he's still controlling her."

With every word I spoke, my anger and frustration increased. The only thing preventing me from doing everything in my power to make that bastard suffer was the miles separating us. But I doubted even that would always prove to be a sufficient barrier. Not when it came to Julia. I'd never felt so damn protective. So out of sorts. And it drove me crazy.

"Well then..." Nikko smirked. "I think you just proved my point."

"What point is that?"

"You care about her. A lot. Probably more than you wish you did."

"I don't—"

"That's a good thing, Lachlan." He squeezed my shoulder, his gesture reassuring. "You deserve this. Especially after everything you went through. After everything you lost. The same goes for her. Maybe you can help her realize that."

I opened my mouth, struggling to come up with a valid response. I would have been lying if I said I hadn't considered what it would be like to have something real with Julia, especially when I made dinner tonight. Or when we baked that cake last night. In those moments, I'd allowed myself to consider the possibility.

But that was all it was... A possibility. A dream. A fantasy.

Not real.

"It will never happen." I pushed away from him, storming back toward the house. "It can't."

I wasn't sure who I was more upset with. Nikko for suggesting the possibility of something real with Julia. Or myself for considering it.

"You have to stop beating yourself up over what happened to Piper, Lachlan."

His words gave me pause. I stopped in my tracks, squeezing my eyes shut as the guilt over that night returned to the surface.

"It wasn't your fault. You're not to blame. You—"

"*Yes, it was!*" I whirled around, eyes on fire, heat scalding my veins. "How can you stand there and say it wasn't!" I bellowed, voice strained and choked with rage and frustration. "It was. *I'm* to blame. *I* failed her. *I* shot her. Me." I pounded a fist against my chest with every word, heart constricting under the weight of the guilt I'd been living with for too long.

"To protect her," Nikko insisted. "You didn't—"

"But I *didn't* protect her!" I roared. "I aimed that gun and fired, knowing full well I could barely see straight after being hit in the head. So you're wrong, Nikko. I *am* to blame. I'm the reason your sister's dead. Not the bastard who broke into our house and raped her. *Me.* And I'm going to have to live with that for the rest of my life. I *deserve* to live with that for the rest of my life. So while I appreciate your little pep talk, this thing with Julia won't go anywhere. It can't. I won't allow it. She deserves better than someone like me."

I spun around, my entire body vibrating with anger and regret as I hurried back up to the house, wanting nothing more than to return to Julia and the bubble we created for ourselves where none of our past trauma or guilt could find us, even if for just a brief moment.

"You deserve better than someone like you, too, ya know," Nikko called out when I was halfway up the stone path.

I paused, but didn't look back at him.

"At least better than this person you've turned into. What's it going to take for you to finally realize that?"

I blinked, opening my mouth to formulate some sort of response. But none came.

Instead, I waved him off and continued walking, not wanting to admit that maybe he was right.

CHAPTER THIRTEEN

Julia

I stared, eyes wide, unable to move, to breathe, to so much as think as Lachlan's confession echoed around me.

I shouldn't have come out here. Should have stayed inside. But when I heard raised voices, I wanted to make sure everything was okay.

But nothing could have prepared me for the conversation I'd stumbled upon.

Lachlan shot Piper.

It wasn't her attacker.

It was Lachlan.

The anguish in his voice as he insisted he didn't deserve to be happy because of his actions that night nearly broke my heart. It was one thing to lose someone you loved. But to live with the guilt you had something to do with it, regardless that you did it in the hopes of protecting her, *saving* her... I couldn't imagine how that must have messed with his mind.

How it *still* messed with his mind.

The blame I'd carried since I learned the truth about Nick still affected me. The "what ifs" still tortured me.

What if I hadn't allowed my fear to control me?

What if I hadn't allowed Nick to manipulate me?

What if I'd raised my suspicions earlier?

How many women would still be alive right now?

I couldn't imagine what Lachlan still endured for his role in Piper's death, knowing the part he played in it.

At the sound of approaching footsteps, my heart ricocheted into my throat. I quickly snapped back to the present, about to hurry into the house, but before I could, Lachlan appeared around the corner, coming to an abrupt stop when he saw me standing there.

He studied me, lips parting as he remained momentarily dumbstruck, unsure of what to say. I had no idea what to say, either.

"You heard." He finally cut through the silence, his words more of a statement than a question.

I simply nodded in response.

"Julia, I..." He shook his head. "I don't know what—"

Before he could finish, I strode to him, pressing my mouth to his, trying to show him that his past didn't matter. That it wasn't his fault.

That, despite the guilt burdening him, he still deserved happiness.

Even if it wasn't with me.

He stiffened, obviously confused as to why I'd want to be with him after overhearing how much of a monster he was. At least in his mind. But I didn't see him that way. I saw his darkness and embraced it.

Because it mirrored my own.

"Kiss me," I begged.

He yanked my body against his and pressed his mouth harder against mine, coaxing my lips open. His hand went to my head, fingers burrowing into my hair, locking me in place.

Desperation and fury dripped from him as he kissed me with hunger. With fervor. With grief. The grief I felt nearly tore me apart to the point I couldn't help but fall into him. To succumb to him.

To surrender to him.

"I'm yours," I murmured, sensing he needed to feel some sort of power or control.

"Mine," he growled, tightening his hold, as if worried I'd disappear.

"Yours."

"Mine."

He kissed me, bruising and biting, stealing my breath and chipping away at my heart.

Hand on my hip, he walked me back into the house, kicking the door closed behind him. Neither one of us came up for air, wanting to drown in each other until we had nothing left to give. When the back of my legs hit the dining room table, he lifted me up, setting me onto the surface.

He ran his fingers up my leg, his frenzied and needy motions a stark contrast to the practiced ministrations from last night.

But I didn't care.

Tonight, I'd happily give him whatever he sought.

Whatever he craved.

Whatever he needed to extinguish the heartache, even if for only a moment.

"Feel me," I whispered, spreading my legs. "Take me." I ran my fingers through his hair, pulling him toward me, his unshaven jawline scratching the sensitive skin of my neck. "Use me."

He groaned, the sound a combination of riotous need and gut-wrenching anguish. Then he brought his eyes to mine, a silent question passing between us, asking if I was sure about this. I simply spread my legs wider, lifting my skirt to my waist, giving him permission to take me any way he desired.

His lips collided with mine, desperate and demanding. I succumbed to his kiss, moaning when his finger ghosted against my center. But it was a tease of a touch. I needed more.

With frantic hands, I reached for his belt, making quick work of removing it. As I was about to unbutton his shorts, he grabbed my wrists, stopping me. He tore his lips away, eyes searching mine.

In one swift move, he hooked his arm around my waist and pulled me to my feet, spinning me around. When he forced my stomach flush with the table, lust coiled within, my heart hammering a thunderous rhythm as I remained in this position, completely exposed and at his mercy.

But I liked it.

More than I thought I would.

He ran a lithe, delicate finger up my inner thigh. My anticipation grew with every drawn-out second. When he toyed with my clit, inserting a finger inside me, I closed my eyes, basking in the euphoria only this man could give me.

His body hovered over mine, teeth tugging on my earlobe, breath scalding my neck as he continued teasing me.

"Is this okay? This position?"

"Y-yes."

"Good." He straightened, the familiar sound of a zipper cutting through the silence. "Because I really need you like this."

When he brought his thick erection up to me, I moaned, an urgent desperation in my voice and movement.

"Do you need me, love?"

"Yes," I whimpered, circling against him, craving him like an addict yearning for her next hit. And that was what Lachlan was. A potent drug I was happily addicted to.

His breath was on my neck again, flaming the inferno growing inside me. "Tell me," he growled.

"I need you, Lachlan. Need to feel you. Need your darkness. And your pain. Give it all to me."

Releasing an animalistic growl, he thrust into me. The sudden invasion made me to scream out in surprise and relief at the same time.

"Okay?" he asked, concerned.

I took a moment to acclimate myself to his size. Then I nodded, glancing over my shoulder, gaze unwavering. "Harder."

His grip on my hip tightened, jaw hardening, pupils dilating as my response hung heavy in the air between us.

As if the sexual tension in the room hadn't been thick and tumultuous before, it was now even more so. More turbulent. More violent.

"Face forward."

His demand sent a chill through me, stomach clenching, heart pounding.

I followed his command, turning my eyes ahead, my breaths coming quickly as I waited for his next move. He drove into me again, this time more savage and unforgiving than before, fingers digging into my skin. I screamed, chest heaving, soul singing.

"Too much?" he asked, peppering kisses along my shoulder blades, the tenderness of his mouth a complete change from the brutality and viciousness with which he just drove into me.

I took several deep breaths, eyes squeezed shut. Then I shook my head. "Harder."

"Fuck," he hissed, his own heavy pants echoing around us. He retreated once more, thumb deftly rubbing my clit, my pleasure increasing with every practiced ministration.

Then he plunged into me, our cries intermingling. This time, he didn't stop, driving into me over and over. Deeper. Harder. Faster.

I clenched and unclenched my fists, struggling to find something to hold onto. Something to keep me grounded when it felt like my soul had left my body, the bliss almost too much for me to handle.

Lachlan ran his hands down my arms, fingers linking with mine, keeping me locked in place as he moved faster, using me to chase away his sorrow.

As he chased away mine.

He nipped at my skin, the ache invigorating, making me want more.

"Harder," I begged. "Bite me harder."

I didn't know what came over me. I'd never been this vocal during sex. About my wants and desires.

But with Lachlan, it felt natural. Like I could tell him what I wanted without worrying he'd judge me. Instead, he'd do everything he could to fulfill my fantasies.

He hesitated, not wanting to hurt me.

"Please. I need it."

Unable to deny me, he clamped onto my neck, the pain nearly blinding. But it was no match for the pleasure shooting through me, the combination of his teeth on me, body over me, and erection inside me pushing me over the edge. I detonated around him, crying out as waves of euphoria filled me.

"Fuck, Julia," he grunted, hands going to my hips as he increased his motions to a scintillating pace, prolonging my pleasure with every thrust. He was ruthless and determined as he chased his own orgasm, his own feeling of bliss, until he released a strangled groan. Giving a final jerk, he collapsed on top of me, our heavy breaths surrounding us, my body still tingling from the aftereffects.

After several moments, he straightened, helping me upright, as well. I opened my mouth, about to make some lame joke to cut through the tension, but before I could, he pulled my body to his.

I didn't have it in me to fight him, to insist on running to the bathroom to clean up, especially when I felt the evidence of his desire trickling down my leg. Just as I knew he needed to feel powerful and in control minutes ago, I knew he needed this now.

"Forgive me," he murmured against my hair.

I sighed, relishing in his embrace. "I don't need to forgive you. I accept you, Lachlan. Faults and all."

He exhaled a breath, holding me tighter than anyone ever had.

CHAPTER FOURTEEN

Julia

I blinked my eyes open after a buzzing stirred me from sleep, Wes' name flashing on my phone from the bedside table. It wasn't yet six in the morning in Hawaii. And while it was nearly noon in Atlanta, a completely reasonable time to call to catch up, I had a feeling that wasn't the purpose of this phone call. Not after last night.

Propping myself up, I brought my phone to my ear.

"Morning, Wes," I answered softly, trying to sound as awake as possible after spending most of the night falling victim to Lachlan's incredible sexual prowess.

After the interlude on the dining room table, things returned to some semblance of normalcy. We roasted marshmallows by the fire pit. Had s'mores. Laughed and joked, as if Lachlan's world hadn't immeasurably shifted only hours ago.

I was more than aware we were both in deep denial. But when I was with him, I was happy. And didn't I deserve to be happy for what little time together we had left?

Didn't he deserve that, too?

"What the hell is going on over there, Jules?" Wes barked out.

"What do you mean?"

"I just got off the phone with Agent Curran. After we spoke the other night... I don't know. There's got to be more to all these creepy gifts you're receiving, considering it's been over five years since Nick went to prison. So I called him to share my concerns. Imagine my surprise when he informed me that not only has new information come to light, but you're somehow involved in putting the pieces together! What the hell, Julia? Why didn't you tell me? We don't keep secrets from each other. Not anymore. Not after—"

"I'm sorry, Wes," I uttered in an attempt to placate him and put him at ease.

It didn't matter we were both in our forties. He'd always be the protective older brother who came to my defense when any of the kids at my new school made fun of me for being adopted. That didn't go away with age.

"The last twenty-four hours have been a whirlwind," I explained. "Hell, the last *thirty-six* hours have been crazy."

A hand on my forearm tore my attention away from my brother and to the man in my bed.

"You okay?" Lachlan asked, concern filling his gaze.

"Hold on a sec, Wes," I said, then put the phone on mute. "It's my brother. He spoke to Agent Curran this morning. It appears Nikko has already reached out to him. Agent Curran mentioned something to Wes, so it's time to fill my brother in about all this shit."

A lazy smile teased Lachlan's lips as he attempted to pull me toward him. "You're adorable when you swear."

I laughed, wanting nothing more than to crawl under the covers with him and tune out the world around us. I loved when he was like this. Playful. Flirtatious. Uninhibited.

It was *easier* when he was like this.

It was those intense moments when he peered at me with heat and want that scared me. That made me question everything.

That made me want this to be real.

"Give me a few minutes." Swatting Lachlan's hand away, I slipped out of bed and grabbed my robe, tightening the sash around my waist. "Then I'll come back and treat you to some more swear words." I unmuted the call, bringing my cell back to my ear.

"I like the sound of that," Lachlan stated as I disappeared out onto the lanai.

"Sorry about that," I said to Wes as I lowered myself

into the lounge chair, drawing in a comforting breath of the fragrant, Hawaiian air.

"Did I hear a man's voice in the background?"

His question wasn't accusatory. More curious than anything.

"I..." I stared ahead, an excuse on the tip of my tongue.

I could tell him I ran out to grab a coffee and it was just one of the other customers. But I didn't see how I could tell Wes everything I'd learned about the jewelry without bringing up Lachlan.

As we learned last night, our lives were now irrevocably connected.

"Yes." I straightened my spine, my voice even. "You did."

The line was silent for a beat as I chewed on my lower lip, wondering what he was thinking, how he was processing what I could only imagine to be somewhat shocking news.

Then I heard what sounded like a hand hitting a desk. "Well, it's about dang time. Who is it? Anyone I know? Someone from corporate?"

I laughed to myself at the irony. My brother was a die-hard Atlanta fan. Had season tickets. So he most certainly knew *of* Lachlan.

"His name is Lachlan Hale," I answered very matter-of-factly.

"No shit? There's a pitcher for Atlanta whose name is Lachlan Hale. Actually, he's been all over the news lately because his sister just..." He trailed off, neither one of us saying anything for several seconds.

I could practically hear the wheels spinning in Wes' head as he put the pieces together. My brother was exceedingly smart. He'd attended Harvard, for crying out loud. Now he was one of the most sought-after architects in the country, if not the world. The instant I mentioned Lachlan's name, I should have expected it wouldn't take long for him to figure it out.

"Jules...," Wes began, a teasing quality to his voice. "What's going on?"

It reminded me of how he sounded when he caught me sneaking in after curfew. Or in the hallway outside our father's study after I picked the lock and stole some of his expensive whiskey. Or under the bleachers during football games with a bag of something that looked alarmingly like marijuana.

"How much time do you have?" I joked.

"For you, Julia, all the time in the world. You know that."

"That I do."

Over next several minutes, I told Wes everything that had happened since my first morning here when I decided to take a stroll along the beach. How I stepped on a jellyfish and Lachlan came to my rescue. How we kept running into each other. About the night we spent talking on the beach. About the arrangement we made to spend the week together, then walk away. How neither of us knew each other's real names, using names we came up with for each other instead. How I learned who he was when I was at the studio yesterday and saw a news piece on his sister's death.

Then how I recognized his sister as the woman who'd approached me last week. How I'd refused to listen to her, desperate to protect Imogene from enduring any more pain because of Nick's actions. How, hours later, Claire was found dead of an apparent suicide. How I originally thought Lachlan knew who I was and had only agreed to sleep with me in the hopes of finding out the information I refused to tell his sister.

How I was wrong.

Then I shared what Claire had uncovered. How the suicides coincided with the dates of death of Nick's victims. How Claire and Ethan believed someone who idolized or admired Nick was doing this. And how I showed Lachlan a photo of the necklace I'd just received, as well as the one received around this time five years ago, and he easily identified both — one as belonging to his sister, the other belonging to his former girlfriend.

When I was about to explain who Piper was and what happened to her, Wes cut me off.

"I know all about what happened to Piper Kekoa. It was messed up. Lachlan had just been promoted to the majors after pitching a no-hitter. Went home to Hawaii to celebrate, and *bam*. His entire life was destroyed in the matter of minutes."

I closed my eyes, heart squeezing at the reminder. I'd

been through a lot of shit. But just thinking about what Lachlan had endured the past few years tore me apart. Not to mention the knowledge that he was the one who ultimately pulled the trigger.

It was no wonder he was so closed off. Why he was a bit of an *arse*, as he put it, when we first met. If I'd lost as many people as he had, I'd probably be angry, too.

But I hadn't really seen that Lachlan since the night on the beach, drinking Opus One from the bottle. Even last night, as upset and frustrated as he was about facing the ghosts of his past, he wasn't bitter. Wasn't hostile. Wasn't distant. I liked to think that maybe I had something to do with that, even though everything inside me told me I shouldn't even entertain the notion.

"So what's the deal with you guys?" Wes pressed. "Is this the real thing?"

"Nah," I said dismissively, hoping he couldn't pick up on any reluctance on my part. "Like I told you. We made an agreement. One week, then we walk away. That hasn't changed."

"Do you like him, though?"

"What do you take me for, dear brother? Some floozy who'd sleep with anything with a pulse?" I joked. "I may have just turned forty, but I still have standards." I played up my Southern drawl a tad, although he probably didn't notice. His was even more pronounced than mine, but in a dignified sort of way that was quintessential Atlanta society.

"If you think I don't know what you're trying to do, using humor to avoid answering the question, you'd better think again."

I was about to argue to the contrary, when he continued.

"I know you, Julia Blaire Prescott. You tend to make jokes when discussing things you'd rather not. But you don't have to do that around me. So... Do. You. Like. Him?"

I sighed, laughing slightly at the mere idea. But I couldn't deny the truth.

"I do, Wes. I know what you're probably thinking," I added quickly. "That he's twenty-seven and I just turned forty."

"I wasn't thinking that at all. Actually..." He chuckled slightly. "I was more hoping you'd be able to pull some strings so I could hit a few balls in the stadium."

I burst out laughing. I could always count on my brother to make light of a difficult situation.

"But seriously, Jules," he said once our laughter died down, his voice sincere. "I don't think there's anything wrong with the age difference. Love is...ageless. If he makes you happy, that's all that should matter." He paused. "*Are* you happy?"

I looked to the sky, giving his question serious consideration as I thought back over the past few days.

"Not much in my life has ever made sense," I began. "It's like I've spent most my life on a train platform, waiting for a train that'll never come. But with him..."

"He put the train in your station?" he said mischievously. "In more ways than one?"

"Wes!" I exclaimed, unable to stop the giggles from overtaking me. "You're my brother! *I'm* the one who's supposed to make inappropriate sex jokes. Not you."

"True. But that was when *I* was the one in need of relationship advice. At least according to you."

"And you were."

"And now *you're* the one who needs it."

I exhaled a long breath, leaning back in my chair. "This isn't a relationship. We agreed."

There was a long silence before Wes finally spoke again. "In my line of work, I deal with contracts all the time. More than I care to think about. And do you want to know what I've learned about contracts? About agreements?"

"What's that?"

"Everything is up for renegotiation."

I opened my mouth to argue that it wasn't possible in our case, then snapped it shut. It wasn't worth it. Wes would never truly understand. He wasn't there. Didn't see how Nick acted behind closed doors.

Didn't hear the final words he'd uttered when the police finally took him into custody.

"*'Till death do us part, Julia. Till death do us part.'*"

I'd lived with that threat in the back of my mind every day since. Most would consider it inconsequential, the desperate ramblings of a narcissistic sociopath who'd fallen from grace.

Not me.

I knew Nick. He didn't make promises haphazardly. If he gave you his word, he kept it. Too many people had already lost their lives because of my husband.

I wouldn't put anyone else's life at risk.

That was why I couldn't renegotiate. Why I had to walk away.

Not to protect myself. But to protect Lachlan.

It was the only way.

CHAPTER FIFTEEN

Julia

The aroma of bacon assaulted me as I emerged from the bedroom after getting ready for another fun-filled day of promotional events. This time, I had a day packed with influencer meetings, as well as a book signing later in the afternoon. I was already exhausted just thinking about all the "people"-ing ahead of me.

But when I walked into the kitchen and saw Lachlan moving bacon around a frying pan, all my negative thoughts about today quickly disappeared. I hadn't expected him to make me breakfast. The steak last night was a treat. But two meals in a row?

"A girl could certainly get used to his," I remarked, sauntering toward him. "Keep it up, and I'll have to get you an apron of your own."

"Would I have to be naked underneath it, too?" He waggled his brows.

"Well, that's a given."

"I like the way you think, Julia Prescott." He lowered his mouth to mine. I curved into him, running my fingers through his silky hair.

"And I like the way you taste, Lachlan Hale."

Groaning, he deepened the kiss, his tongue swiping against mine briefly before he pulled back.

"Don't distract me, or I'll ruin the bacon and the pig would have been slaughtered in vain."

"We can't have that now, can we?"

"Certainly not." He winked. "Now, how do you like your eggs?"

"Unfertilized, thank you very much."

He laughed as he used a pair of tongs to flip the bacon. "I like this side of you."

Glancing over his shoulder, he met my smile as I made my way to the opposite side of the island and hoisted myself onto the barstool, a glass of orange juice and a steaming cup of coffee waiting for me. To my surprise, it was prepared precisely how I liked it. It was only our second morning together, yet he remembered how I preferred my coffee. Such a little thing. Something most people wouldn't think a big deal.

But for me, it meant he paid attention.

That he listened.

That he cared.

"But seriously." He lifted his eyes to mine. "Over-easy good for your eggs?"

"Perfect."

He beamed, then re-focused on the stovetop, flipping the eggs in the pan with ease.

Bringing my mug to my lips, I took another sip of coffee as I admired him. There was something so normal and domesticated about watching him cook me breakfast. For a moment, I allowed myself to consider what it would be like to have this every day.

To wake up in his arms. To lose myself in him first thing in the morning. To shower together while he treated me to another mind-blowing orgasm. Then to get dressed while he made us breakfast.

The image in my mind was so clear, as if it were reality.

But it could never be mine.

Not with my past.

I wasn't destined to have a happily ever after, especially with someone like Lachlan.

Even if it weren't for Nick, we were at two completely different stages of our lives. I'd already been married. Had a teenage daughter. Could I really expect him to be okay with that? To sacrifice having a family of his own?

He may not think so, but he deserved the life he'd always dreamed of.

He'd never have that with me.

"Hope they're to your liking," Lachlan said as he set my plate in front of me, then sat beside me.

I snapped my gaze to his, forcing out a smile, hoping he didn't pick up on the ache in my heart at just how perfect this was.

And how fleeting it had to be.

"Thank you for this. It's... It's really sweet. I'm usually the one in the kitchen. It's nice to have a break from reality."

"That's what I'm here for." He smiled. "To give you a much-needed break from reality." He held my gaze for a moment, then turned his attention to his eggs.

As we ate, our conversation remained light and easy, despite the warring emotions in my heart. I asked what he planned to do during the day, to which he said he intended to go to Nikko's, since he had a home gym that Lachlan needed to take advantage of in order to maintain his conditioning. And I told him all about my influencer meetings this morning, followed by a book signing in Waikiki later this afternoon.

"Sounds like a busy day."

"It sure does," I responded, floating my eyes to the clock.

Upon spying the time, I jumped to my feet. "Shit. My driver's probably already out front." I smoothed a hand down my dress. "I hate being late."

"I'll clean up around here before I head out." He stood. "What time should I come by tonight?"

"I think my book signing is from four to six, so maybe around seven?"

"Seven it is." He leaned toward me, his lips warm against mine.

With just a simple touch, I couldn't help but hunger for more.

"Seven seems so far away," I murmured.

"Then I'll just have to give you something to hold you over until then." Cupping my head, he pulled me toward him, coaxing my mouth open, his kiss sweet, yet exhilarating at the same time.

"Halle-*fucking*-lujah!"

At the sound of Naomi's voice, I inhaled sharply and jumped away from Lachlan, wiping my mouth in a lackluster attempt to hide the fact she'd caught us making out.

"Oh, stop. It was only a kiss. Now, if I'd walked in on him going down on you, things might be a bit more awkward."

Not missing a beat, she turned her attention to the man at my side.

"Lachlan. Good to see you again. And to call you by your real name. Assuming you two talked last night and didn't just screw until God knows when." She didn't give me a chance to respond before continuing. "And can I take a moment to give you a fucking round of applause?" She clapped slowly. "Seven orgasms? That is damn impressive. You should include that in your baseball stats. ERA. RBI. Who the fuck cares? OAN is much more important."

"OAN?" he asked, confused, seemingly unsure how to handle Naomi.

Welcome to the club.

All I could do was shrug. Naomi was, well... Naomi.

"Orgasm a night."

"I, uh... I'm not sure what to say."

"She's not wrong." I edged toward him. "Seven orgasms in one night *is* damn impressive."

"True." His lips brushed against mine. "And eight was even more so, wasn't it?"

"It certainly was," I admitted, body sparking to life yet again as his mouth moved with mine in a tender kiss.

"*Eight!*" Naomi shrieked. "You've *got* to be kidding me!"

I laughed against Lachlan's mouth, then pulled back.

"It's official. I hate you. I mean, I'm happy for you, but I still hate you." She directed her attention to Lachlan. "Do you have any brothers? Maybe a cousin? Hell, at this point, I'd settle for someone who doesn't think my clit is a scratch-off card, rubbing the damn thing as if it's about to reveal a prize."

"*Naomi!*" I gasped, although I shouldn't have been surprised. She was never one to keep her thoughts to herself, regardless of the subject matter.

"What? It's true! It's a bundle of nerves. Treat it with some love, for crying out loud."

"On *that* note..." I turned toward Lachlan. "I should be going."

He gave me a brilliant smile. "I'll walk you out." He grabbed my bag and, touching his hand to my lower back, led me out of the house and toward the street where my driver, Paul, waited, the back passenger door open.

"See you soon, Lachlan," Naomi sang as she climbed into the car, giving us a few moments of privacy.

"Thanks again for breakfast. And dinner." I lifted myself onto my toes. "And those eight orgasms." I brushed a kiss against his neck, lingering for several moments. "Seven o'clock. Don't be late." Then I lowered myself back to my heels and started to climb into the car.

Unexpectedly, he grabbed my forearm, yanking my body against his, the motion stealing my breath. Before I could ask him what he was doing, his lips were on mine, tempting and teasing in one last, salacious kiss that left me hungry for more.

"Seven o'clock," he growled. Then he spun, striding back up to the house, leaving my stomach fluttering and heart yearning.

"Oh. My. God," Naomi all but squealed when I finally slid into the back seat. "That was... Well, I don't think there's a word in the English language to describe what that was."

I laughed to myself. "You're right about that."

"So..." She nudged me with her elbow. "You worked it all out?"

I drew in a deep breath, attempting to collect my thoughts. I wasn't even sure what to tell her about everything that transpired last night. It was so much to process. But I didn't know how much I *could* tell her, considering a lot of what I learned now appeared to be part of an ongoing investigation. So, instead of disclosing every single detail, I went with the simplest explanation.

"Yes, we worked it all out. You were right. He had no idea who I was. It was all a coincidence."

"Or kismet."

With a smug grin, she crossed her arms in front of her chest and leaned back against the seat. Then she stole a glance my way.

"How about the status quo? Does that stay the same?"

"What do you mean?"

"Your arrangement. Do you still plan to walk away at the end of the week?"

I parted my lips, the myriad of reasons I had for walking away on the tip of my tongue.

But, for the first time, no words came.

CHAPTER SIXTEEN

Lachlan

I shouldn't be here, I thought as I hovered in the aisles of a popular local bookstore, my gaze on Julia as she interacted with the hundreds of fans who'd come out to listen to her speak and get a book signed.

I should have spent the afternoon with Ethan, going over his files to see if we could find a clue we'd overlooked. Something that could help us figure out who was behind this.

But all day, I couldn't stop thinking about Julia.

I'd initially left my mum's house to get a break from the constant reminders of Claire and Piper. But as I drove along the island, I found myself navigating toward Waikiki, to the bookstore where Julia currently signed book after book. My hand cramped just watching her, all too familiar with what that was like.

I had no idea how popular she was. Didn't exactly spend my days following food blogs or watching cooking shows. But when I saw the line snaking around the block, hundreds of people dying to meet her, I couldn't help but smile with pride. More so after watching her interact with her fans the past few hours. They adored her. Were drawn to her.

How could anyone not be, especially when they saw her gorgeous smile or heard her beautiful laugh?

I certainly was.

After lingering in the self-help section longer than any reasonable person should, I noticed the line finally dying down, only one person waiting to meet Julia. I returned the book I'd been pretending to read to the shelf and made my way toward her.

As I approached, one of the employees walked up, most likely about to tell me I was too late. Then his eyes flickered with recognition. I'd hoped no one would recognize me if I wore a baseball cap and sunglasses.

Then again, that was probably *why* he did. If I were in a button-down shirt with my hair styled and face clean shaven, I doubted he would have given me a second glance. Instead, my current appearance wasn't that different from how I looked on the field.

"It's okay." I winked. "She's a friend."

Dumbstruck, he simply nodded, allowing me to stand behind Julia's last fan.

Struggling to reel in my smile as she said goodbye and thanked the woman for coming, I swiped up one of the cookbooks stacked on the display. When she turned my way, her eyes widened, lips parting.

"What are you—"

"Can you sign this for me, please?" I interrupted, placing the book on the high-top table in front of her. Grinning salaciously, I leaned forward, dropping my voice to no louder than a whisper. "I am a huge fan of your humming-bird cake."

A blush bloomed on her cheeks, her heartfelt, addicting laughter filling the space.

God, I loved seeing her like this. Loved seeing her smile. Loved hearing her laugh. And it was even more meaningful knowing I was the source of it.

"And who shall I make it out to?" She flicked her eyes to mine, attempting to maintain the same professionalism she exhibited toward her fans.

I rested my elbow on the table and curved toward her. Her body responded to my proximity, breaths increasing, pupils dilating.

"What would you like to call me?" I murmured seductively.

"I have a few ideas."

With a smirk, she opened to the first page, making sure

to hide what she was writing. When she finished, she closed the cover, handing the book back.

I gave her a smile and cracked it open, admiring her flowing penmanship, a stark contrast to my barely legible chicken scratch.

To my favorite jellyfish expert,

If you enjoy my hummingbird cake, wait until you get a taste of my peach pie. I hear it's quite…addicting.

Yours,

Julia

"Is that an offer, Ms. Prescott?" I asked, closing the book, gaze roaming her dress-clad body, the sweetheart neckline accentuating her chest.

She tilted her head back. "What do you think?"

Desperate for a taste of her, I started to erase the space between us when a loud throat clearing cut through.

Julia stilled, darting her eyes to her left where Naomi stood, brows raised, hands on her hips.

"So nice to see you again, Mr. Hale," Naomi said, her tone exuding a certain level of professionalism I never expected, especially after our rather colorful conversation this morning. "What brings you here today? Or do I even need to ask?"

"I came to steal Julia away." I turned toward her. "Unless you have more to do." I glanced at my watch. "You said this was over at six. I didn't want to wait another hour to see you, so I figured I'd see if I could take you home myself."

"Of course you can 'take her home'." Dropping her serious demeanor, Naomi playfully waggled her brows, giving Julia an overly dramatic wink. "Hell, for all I care, you should 'take her home' all night long."

"On *that* note..." Julia rolled her eyes. "Let's get out of here." She turned toward Naomi. "Do you need help cleaning any of this up?"

"Go!" She practically pushed her toward me. "Enjoy your time in Hawaii. And everything this island has to offer... If you know what I mean."

Julia laughed, cheeks reddening once more as Naomi pulled a large, leather tote bag from beneath the table.

"Here. Now go."

Just as she was about to take the bag from Naomi, I stepped in front of her. "I'll get that."

"Thanks," Julia said with a smile as I slung her bag over my shoulder.

"Ready?" I asked.

"Ready."

Without giving it a second thought, I grasped her hand and started pulling her through the store. She immediately stiffened, stopping in her tracks as she flung her gaze to mine, then to our joined hands. It hadn't even dawned on me that I shouldn't be doing this. That we were in public, in a place where people certainly recognized her. Hell, they'd specifically come out here just for her.

"Sorry," I muttered, quickly dropping my grip, giving her some space so as to not bring any attention to us.

Or at least no more attention than we already had.

But as we continued through the aisles, I felt her fingers slowly link with mine. I snapped my eyes toward her, silently questioning if she were truly okay with this. When she smiled, tightening her hold, a lightness filled me.

I walked proudly beside her, ignoring all the stares as I waited to pay for my cookbook. Once I did, we made our way out of the store and onto the sidewalk, my steps quickening with every second.

"Where are we going in such a hurry?" she asked, struggling to keep up with my long strides as we practically ran around the corner and toward the parking lot.

Coming to an abrupt stop, I yanked her against me. A gasp fell from her throat at the sudden movement. I slammed my lips against hers in a hungry kiss, tongue swiping, teeth clashing.

Instantly, all the tension evaporated from my body, a sense of peace filling me. "I've been dying to do that all bloody day." Burying my head in her neck, I ran my hand along her frame, trying to memorize every curve, knowing in mere days, all I'd have left of her were memories. "You're a goddamn drug, Julia."

She grabbed my face, bringing my lips to within a breath of hers. "Then why don't you take another hit."

I circled my hips against her. "With pleasure." My mouth descended. "With immense pleasure."

CHAPTER SEVENTEEN

Lachlan

"Where are we?" Julia asked as I put my SUV into park, bright lights visible in the distance.

I killed the ignition, turning to her. "Somewhere important to me."

I jumped out of the car, then hurried around to open her door, helping her down. Thankfully, I had the foresight to stop by Julia's house first so she could change. As incredible as she looked in the dress and heels, I wanted her to be comfortable tonight. And in the white, linen sundress, Egyptian-style sandals laced up her legs, hair in loose waves, face relatively free from makeup, she definitely seemed much more at ease.

"'*Hale Field. Home of Little Dreamers Little League*,'" she read through squinted eyes as we neared the field house, the sound of bats hitting balls intermingling with clapping and cheers of encouragement. "What is this?"

"My good deed."

As I led her through an opening in the chain-link fence, two baseball fields came into view, both currently in use.

"Your good deed?" she repeated, looking around in amazement.

"This island may be a paradise to some, but away from the tourist attractions and posh beach houses, there's a lot of poverty. The school dropout rate is high. As is the crime rate. There are a lot of at-risk youth. Kids who, if they learned discipline, learned how to work as a team, might have a chance at a future. So that's what I give them." I gestured at the fields. "An opportunity to play baseball at no cost, other than their time and effort."

Mouth agape and eyes wide, she slowly scanned her surroundings, taking it all in.

I wasn't sure what compelled me to bring her here. For some reason, I wanted her to know this part of me. Didn't want her to only see the Lachlan Hale everyone else knew. Wanted her to understand what made me tick. What drove me to keep doing what I did.

Maybe to see that, despite what she'd learned about me last night regarding the role I played in Piper's death, I was still a good person.

That I was worthy of her forgiveness. Her acceptance.

"How big is your league?" she asked.

"We sponsor twelve teams. We play other leagues on

the island throughout the spring and summer. For most of these kids, baseball is the only good thing in their lives. They were at risk of failing out of school, turning to drugs or crime. But once we got them into baseball, taught them the importance of being a team player, of taking responsibility for their gear and showing up on time, it filtered into all other areas of their life. Kids who could barely muster Cs and Ds were suddenly getting As and Bs. All because of baseball."

With every word I spoke, my passion increased.

"That's something people don't give sports enough credit for. Yes, we tend to glorify these amazing players, myself included. But we all started here. On a field just like this. We all put in thousands of hours of hard work to get to the point where people idolize us. But even without dreams of playing professionally, organized sports can still change a person's life. Look at these kids." I waved my arm at the dozens of teenagers in uniforms, cheering on their teammates, working together to play the best game they could. To "leave it all out on the field", as my high school coach always said.

"All these young men were just one decision away from turning to a life of crime. Now they have bright futures ahead of them.

"And we have the same exact program for girls. A softball program where—"

Before I could finish, Julia flung her arms around me, pressing her lips against mine. Now it was *my* turn to be taken by surprise. But it only lasted a second before I melted into her, savoring in her warmth. Her taste. Her everything.

"The more time I spend with you, the more you surprise me," she confessed.

"Good surprise or bad surprise?"

"Good surprise." She smiled before her expression fell, a vulnerability about her. "And, if I'm being honest, a scary surprise, too."

I cupped her cheek, resting my forehead on hers. "You're a scary surprise, too," I admitted in a rare moment of honesty. But if she was willing to be vulnerable, so was I.

I peered at her, wanting to ask what she was thinking, see where her head was after the events of last night, but before I could, a familiar voice interrupted, bringing back memories of my own early baseball days.

"I heard rumblings through the crowd you were here."

Stepping away from Julia, I looked up as a man wearing a baseball cap and polo shirt bearing the league's logo walked toward us.

"I knew you were on the island, but shit, man. You could have given me a heads-up."

"Sorry, Coop," I offered, taking his hand as he pulled me in for a hug. "It was kind of a last-minute decision."

"No apology necessary. It's good to see you." He pulled back, looking at me with pride. Then he stole a glance at Julia before raising a brow in my direction, obviously surprised to see me with a woman. I couldn't blame him. Considering he'd been like a father to me during my high school years and even after, he was more than aware of my reasons for not dating.

Reasons that Julia seemed to have completely eviscerated last night with her unequivocal acceptance of my truth.

"Daniel Cooper," I said with a smile, "I'd like to introduce you to Julia Prescott."

"Pleasure to meet you." He extended his hand.

Julia grasped it. "You, as well, Daniel."

"Just call me Coop. That's what everyone does."

"Coop runs this league for me," I explained. "But before that he was my high school baseball coach. Encouraged me to sign with Atlanta senior year when they sent a recruiter out to watch me pitch. Hell, he was the one who insisted their recruiters make the trip all the way out here in the first place."

"Because coming to Hawaii is *such* a burden," Julia shot back playfully, eliciting a chuckle from Coop.

"Still, I owe it all to him. I wouldn't be where I am if he weren't a stubborn son of a bitch who doesn't take no for an answer."

"Believe me." He placed his hand on my shoulder, squeezing. "Your debt is more than repaid." He nodded toward the fields, which caused Julia to look at me quizzically.

"When I was in high school," I began, "Coop would

raise funds so our team could sponsor a few kids who showed talent, yet couldn't afford to play."

"It wasn't much." Coop shrugged. "But baseball definitely changed my life. I wanted to repay the favor."

"That's a beautiful gesture," Julia offered.

"Once this guy hit it big...," Coop slapped my back, "he took my idea and expanded on it. Because of him, we've helped hundreds of kids. Even got a couple dozen of them full scholarships to play baseball in college, something they never would have been able to do otherwise. For those who aren't lucky enough to score a full ride through baseball, we award a full undergraduate scholarship every year to two of our players who exhibit exceptional educational achievement." He hitched a thumb in my direction. "All thanks to Lachlan."

Blinking, Julia darted her gaze to mine. "*You* pay their college tuition?"

I opened my mouth, about to tell her it wasn't that big a deal, when Coop interjected.

"And books. And board. And a stipend for living expenses. One female and one male every year."

"Wow. I'm..." Julia stared at me in amazement, as if seeing a completely different side of me. In a way, I suppose she was. "Well, I don't know what to say. That's...incredible."

"Lachlan's one of the best people I've ever met," Coop said proudly. "You snagged yourself a real catch."

I was about to tell Coop it wasn't like that, that we weren't together, when Julia sent a smile my way.

"I'm starting to realize that." She held her hand toward mine.

Something passed between us as I linked my fingers with hers. An understanding of sorts. An awareness. An acceptance.

"Come on. Let's go watch some baseball." Coop patted my back, walking with us toward one of the fields.

"Now, tell me, Julia. What's your favorite team?"

Stealing a sly glance at me, her mouth curved up in the corners. "I'm slowly becoming a big fan of Atlanta."

He chuckled, giving me a knowing look. "I thought so."

CHAPTER EIGHTEEN

Julia

"Sorry that took so long," Lachlan said as he climbed up the now empty bleachers, where I'd been sitting for the better part of the past hour, simply watching Lachlan as he signed everything thrust in front of him. Baseballs. Jerseys. Hats. You name it, he signed it.

Once the games ended and word got out that the benefactor of the league and star pitcher, Lachlan Hale, had made a surprise appearance, everyone lined up in the hopes of meeting him and getting his autograph. And Lachlan didn't hesitate to talk to anyone who wanted to meet him, interacting with the kids as if it were second nature.

"No need to apologize." I stared into his brilliant, blue eyes as he lowered himself beside me on the bench. "This was... It was exactly what I needed."

A small smile on his lips, the man beside me barely resembled the brooding surfer I met mere days ago. He seemed lighter. Less angry. Less...burdened.

"It's good to come home once in a while. Remember where I came from."

His gaze swept over the empty fields as he drew in a deep breath.

I did the same, wanting to know what he smelled. Fresh-cut grass. Raw earth. Leather.

The aroma of baseball.

I had a feeling I'd forever associate this scent with him.

"Australia isn't home?" I asked.

He thought for a beat, brows furrowed in contemplation. Then he shook his head. "I don't think it ever really was. As I mentioned, my mum's Hawaiian. Even though she married an Australian with Scottish roots—"

"Hence the name," I joked.

"Yeah." He ran his fingers through his hair, smirking. "I mean, Lachlan *is* a pretty popular name in Australia. Probably because there are a lot of Scottish people there. But despite the fact I spent the first thirteen years of my life thousands of miles away from here, Mum made sure I knew about the culture. Knew my heritage. So when we came to live here after my father passed away, well... It felt like I was finally home. When Piper died..." He shook his head, voice catching.

I covered his hand with mine and squeezed. When he lifted his eyes to mine, I gave him a reassuring smile.

An accepting smile.

"Well, I left. Didn't think this place would ever feel like home again. Hell, this is the first time I'm even seeing all of this." He waved at the ball fields in front of us. "I couldn't stomach being back on this island, regardless of how important this league is to me. But now..."

"Yes?"

His lips curved, a peaceful expression crossing his face. Reaching out, he pushed a wayward curl behind my ear, cupping my cheek. "Now I feel like I've finally found my home after years of searching."

I opened my mouth, unsure how to respond to that. I couldn't ignore the hidden meaning in his words. The heat and intensity in his gaze making it clear he wasn't just talking about being back on this island, but something more.

Something that should have scared me more than it did.

"Come on." Standing, he extended his hand. I happily placed mine in his. "The night's not over yet." He winked, pulling me down the bleachers before turning toward me. "Wait here a second."

"Okay."

Releasing my hand, he jogged toward the field house where it looked like Cooper was locking things up for the night. I watched as they talked for a minute. Then Lachlan disappeared into the shed-like building, emerging several moments later with something that resembled an equipment bag slung over his shoulder.

After giving Cooper a brief nod, Lachlan made his way back to me.

"What's going on?" I asked, eyeing the bag.

"We're going to have a little fun."

Wrapping his hand around mine, he led me across the wide expanse of grass to the opposite side of the field. As we walked, I kept stealing glances at him, unable to stop admiring him.

Less than forty-eight hours ago, I had no idea who he was, other than someone to have fun with while I was here.

Now I couldn't picture him as anyone other than a baseball player. Seeing him under the bright lights, an equipment bag over his shoulder... It suited him. Like this was where he was meant to be. What he was born to do.

When we approached a caged-in section of the field, Lachlan retrieved a set of keys from his pocket. After unlocking the padlock, he pushed the gate open, gesturing for me to enter in front of him. I stared at him curiously, but entered nonetheless, watching as he rummaged through the equipment bag, pulling out a helmet.

"Put this on."

"Why?"

"To protect your head." He gestured at a pitching machine at the far end of the cage, netting surrounding it.

"You want me to...hit?"

"Just humor me. Figured it would be fun to do something different."

"I haven't swung a bat since high school."

He tilted his head, crossing his arms over his chest, muscles straining against the sleeves of his t-shirt. It took everything I had to not reach out and touch them. A shiver of excitement rushed through me at the reminder that I was lucky enough to know what those muscles felt like. To fall asleep with those arms wrapped around me.

At least for another few days.

"You played?" Lachlan asked, forcing my gaze away from his biceps.

"Mainly to piss off my mother who didn't consider softball to be a sport becoming of a proper Southern debutante." I played up my accent.

"You just shot up a thousand spots on the hot scale. I mean, you were off the charts before, but now…" He sucked on his bottom lip, gaze raking over me in a way that made me feel like he was mentally undressing me.

"Why? Because of my accent?"

"No." An arm going around my waist, he dragged my body against his. "Because you played softball. Second base?"

My brows furrowed. "How'd you know? Did Naomi—"

"Your height. Short people do great there. Quick toss to first. Not a bad distance over to third if making a double play. I can tell you one thing. You certainly wouldn't be at first base, short stuff." He playfully swatted my ass, dropping his hold. "Now, let's see what you remember." He extended the helmet toward me.

Feigning annoyance, I took it from him, smoothing my

hair back as I put it on my head. It was a little big, but would serve its purpose. After testing out a few of the bats, I selected one that felt the best and made my way toward the plate.

"If I make a complete fool out of myself, don't laugh. Please. It's been twenty years since I've picked up a bat."

"Interesting. The first time I picked up a bat *was* twenty years ago."

I placed a hand on my hip, frowning. "Probably not the smartest thing to say to someone holding a bat."

"Probably not."

Smirking, he placed a helmet on his head, then walked to the pitching machine and ducked underneath the netting, turning it on, a whirring sound filling the night sky.

I dug my back foot into the dirt, bending my knees slightly as I brought the bat behind me, focused on the pitching machine.

"And, for the record," Lachlan stated, "you look fucking hot holding that bat."

"Apron and heels hot?" I shot back.

"Oh, I'm absolutely picturing you in the apron and heels. *And* the helmet and bat."

I burst out laughing. "You are so twisted."

"Just keeping it interesting for you, beautiful. Now, you ready?" He retrieved a ball from the basket beside the machine and held it up.

I returned to some semblance of a batting stance. "Ready as I'll ever be."

He nodded, eyes locked on mine as he dropped the ball into the chute. I did my best to not look at him and focus on the ball as it flew toward me. But it wasn't enough, my swing not even close to connecting.

"It's okay. Now you know what the pitch looks like. It's why you're never supposed to swing on the first pitch."

"Got it."

I brought the bat behind me once again, my attention on the machine instead of Lachlan. But, despite preparing myself the best I could, I still couldn't even manage to graze my bat against the ball.

"Don't be timid," Lachlan encouraged, ducking under the netting and jogging toward me. "You have a really good stance, but you second-guess yourself. Don't do that. Once you decide to go after something, you have to go all-in."

"All-in?"

"Here. Let me show you what I mean." He stood behind me, hands covering mine on the grip of the bat. Then he led me through the motions, my body a puppet as he swung.

I tried to focus on what he was showing me, but all I could think about was how amazing his body felt against mine. How confident and assured his motions were. No hesitation. No uncertainty.

"There," he said after the fifth or sixth repetition of the swing. "You're getting the hang of it. Now, try it on your own. Follow through and snap your wrists at the end."

"We really don't have to do this, Lachlan. I can just watch you hit. I'm sure you're infinitely better than I am."

"You showed me how to bake a cake. It's *my* turn to teach *you* something. Share part of myself with you." He narrowed his gaze, almost pleading to let him do this.

I couldn't say no to him when he looked at me like that.

Hell, I doubted I could say no to him even when he didn't, but knowing he was going through all this just to share a piece of himself with me, a piece he rarely gave to anyone, touched me on a deeper level.

So, instead of trying to get out of this, I returned to my batting stance, all my concentration fixated on that pitching machine and hitting the ball.

I flexed my hands, bouncing slightly as I waited, the seconds seeming to stretch. When I heard the *whoosh* of the ball leaving the machine, I held my breath, dropped my shoulder, and swung. But instead of worrying about whether I'd hit it or not, I did what Lachlan instructed.

As I snapped my wrists, the most miraculous thing happened. My bat actually connected with the ball, a crack sounding from the metal.

Then the sky.

I straightened, peering into the distance just as lightning streaked across the sky, another boom echoing.

"Looks like that's our cue to leave," Lachlan remarked, powering down the pitching machine and heading toward me.

"Probably a good idea." I handed him the bat, then

removed the helmet. "Wouldn't want any of those baseballs turning into a pile of string like in *The Natural*."

He gave me an amused look. "You've seen *The Natural*?"

"It was actually one of my favorite movies growing up. Something about it always resonated with me. About an underdog winning the game."

"And someone who was a little older getting a second chance." Lachlan reminded me of one of the movie's central plots. How the main character was considered past his prime when he was brought up to play in the majors but didn't let his age stop him. How he found his happiness.

He pushed a few tendrils of hair behind my ear, cupping my cheek. "It's never too late for a second chance, Julia."

I peered into his eyes, unsure how to interpret his words. Was he simply saying that because I'd just celebrated a milestone birthday, one he was fully aware I struggled with?

Or because he wanted me to take a chance on him?

Could I take a chance on him? On me? On us?

Fat droplets of rain fell on my head as the sky opened up, quickly drenching everything.

But that didn't seem to bother Lachlan. In fact, he craned his head back, drawing in a deep breath. "God, I love the smell of a Hawaiian thunderstorm."

I watched him, a look of serenity and peace washing over him as he basked in the rain hitting his face. He seemed so carefree, the weight burdening him lately nowhere to be found. Like he'd finally let go of the ghosts keeping him tethered to the past.

If he could let go of his past so easily, why couldn't I?

When another bolt of lightning lit up the sky, he snapped his head forward. "But as much as I love the smell, being outside while it's lightning probably isn't the safest thing. Come on."

He quickly finished putting everything into the equipment bag and zipped it up, slinging it over his shoulder. My hand enclosed in his, we jogged across the field, the steady rain increasing with every passing moment. My hair was stuck to my face, sundress clinging to my skin...

Yet I didn't care.

I should have hated this. Soaked to the bone, hair a mess, sundress muddy as we sprinted toward the field house. But none of that mattered. Being out in the rain with Lachlan was...freeing.

When we finally reached the equipment shed, Lachlan made quick work of the lock, heaving the door open. Slipping inside, he dropped the equipment bag with a thud, both of us panting as we attempted to catch our breath, rain dripping off our bodies.

His gaze briefly dropped to my heaving chest that didn't leave much to the imagination now that my sundress was soaked through. As his eyes returned to mine, heat swirled within, the atmosphere instantly shifting.

I didn't have a chance to brace myself before he

advanced, backing me up against the wall, his lips crashing against mine in a searing kiss I felt from the top of my head to the tips of my toes.

I melted into him, wrapping my arms around his neck, tugging him as close as possible. But no matter how close he was, it wasn't enough.

It would never be enough.

He was my drug. My remedy.

My perfect addiction.

"Lachlan," I moaned as I hooked a leg around his waist, pulsing and craving.

"What the bloody hell are you doing to me?" He peppered kisses along my collarbone as his hand roamed to my leg, hitching up the skirt of my dress.

When his fingers dipped beneath my panties, I released a cry of relief, moving against him, needing to feel him. To lose myself in him. To drown in him, never to resurface again.

Hand hooking into the side of my panties, a sharp burn shot through me as he ripped them from my body. I yelped, but any momentary pain was replaced with desire when he pushed down his shorts and brought his erection up to me.

Our gazes locked before he thrust into me, my eyes going wide as he filled me to the hilt. He stilled for several moments, neither of us moving as we basked in this sensation.

Then he exhaled, slowly retreating before driving back into me. But this time, he didn't stop. He thrust over and over again, relentless and unforgiving as he chased what he needed.

As he gave me precisely what I needed.

And that was the hard truth I now had to accept.

Lachlan was exactly what I needed. But was that a good enough reason to stay?

To put his life at risk?

I didn't know if I could stomach the thought of having any more blood on my hands.

And there wasn't a single doubt in my mind.

If Nick found out about him, there would most certainly be blood.

CHAPTER NINETEEN

Lachlan

The aroma of lavender and vanilla seeped its way into my subconscious as I stirred from sleep, more rested and sated than I thought possible after that fateful phone call a week ago.

It was surreal to think it had only been a week since I spent the night in jail before Brett bailed me out, instructing me to go home to Hawaii to be with family. It seemed like a lifetime had passed since then, but also like I blinked and it was suddenly a week later.

Especially considering in just two days, Julia would board a flight to Atlanta and our time together would be over.

Our agreement would be over.

One moment, I was convinced it was for the best. Our lives were too complicated. All rationale and reason told me Julia would only end up being a bigger distraction than she already was. And the absolute last thing I needed in my life right now was a distraction.

But in those quiet moments, when we brushed our teeth together, or cooked together, or even sat on the couch and read together, I found myself entertaining the possibility of more.

Was it even a possibility, though?

I wasn't sure.

"I can feel you thinking," she murmured, voice husky with sleep.

"You can *feel* me thinking?" I mused, pulling her closer and peppering kisses along her shoulder blade.

"I sure can, Mr. Hale."

"How so, Ms. Prescott?" I teased back, hand skimming her frame, her skin so soft and smooth.

"I can't explain it." She rolled over, meeting my gaze. She ran her hand through my hair, her touch lighting me on fire. "I just can."

God, she was gorgeous first thing in the morning — eyes heavy from sleep, hair tangled from sex.

"Okay. You got me. I was thinking."

"About?"

"You." I lowered my mouth to hers. "Always you."

At the gentle brushing of my lips against hers, she

moaned, our tongues touching in a sweet kiss. It wasn't the carnal, lust-filled exchange that typically accompanied our more passionate moments. But it still drove me wild.

My heart squeezed over the notion of never again experiencing her kisses once she left Hawaii. Which confused me.

Before Julia, I didn't give much thought to the women I invited into my bed. They were there to serve a purpose. To make me forget.

While Julia certainly helped me forget, she also helped me forgive, the guilt I'd been carrying no longer as heavy a burden.

All in just a week's time.

"What exactly were you thinking?" she asked when I brought our kiss to an end.

I pushed a few tendrils of hair behind her ear. "About Monday," I confessed.

Her expression fell, a sad smile pulling on her lips.

Over the past few days, I sensed her struggling with our original agreement, especially with all the time we'd spent exploring my favorite spots on the island. The Mermaid Caves. The Botanical Gardens. Hell, I stole her away from her commitments yesterday and all we did was stroll through the farmer's market, something I normally hated doing. But with her, it was new and exciting.

That was the thing about Julia. It didn't matter what we did. Everything was exhilarating when I was with her.

Better.

Brighter.

"We still have all day tomorrow," she reminded me.

As much as I would love to convince her to play hooky today, too, spend as much time together as possible, I couldn't. It was the grand opening of the new location of her bakery. She had to be there.

"And most of the day Monday," she continued. "And don't forget about tonight." Her expression turned flirtatious as she waggled her brows.

"Yeah? Any ideas what you'd like to do tonight?" I traced a circle along her hip, addicted to her soft skin.

"I have a few."

"Any you care to share? You know. Solely for educational purposes," I teased with a smirk. "Make sure it's something I'm interested in."

"Oh, I'm pretty sure you'll be interested." Her eyes briefly dropped to my waist, my erection hard.

I leaned toward her, lips skimming hers, needing her once more before I was forced to go all day without her.

"Show me."

Eyes dark with desire, she pushed me onto my back and straddled me. When her heat pulsed against me, my erection hardened even more. I gripped her hips, desperate to feel her. To lose myself in her. To fall into her.

Biting her lower lip, she wrapped her hand around my arousal, teasing and tempting. Then she lifted herself up before gradually lowering onto me.

"Goddamn," I groaned at the sensation of her warmth, so addictive and inviting.

She moved slowly, sensually, her hair framing us, blocking out everything but us and this incredible feeling only she could give me.

CHAPTER TWENTY

Lachlan

"And to what do we owe this unexpected surprise?" *Eme* remarked the instant I stepped into The Shack on Saturday morning to meet Nikko for breakfast.

"*Aloha, Eme.*" I smiled at the short, naturally tan woman as she approached. I bent, pressing my forehead to hers in greeting.

"You come see me when you first land on the island, then nothing for days," she chided. "I thought you'd vanished and it would be another five years until I saw you again."

I shrugged sheepishly, running my hand through my hair. "I'm sorry. I've been...pre-occupied."

"Is that what you kids call it now?" She nudged me

with her elbow, winking slyly. "I heard Nikko say you met a girl. Is it true?"

"It's nothing." My smile wavered, words lacking any semblance of conviction.

This thing with Julia *was* supposed to be nothing. But what about now? Was it still nothing after spending a week together? Sharing our scars, our hopes, our fears?

More importantly, did I *still want* it to be nothing?

"If you say so, Lochie."

"We're just hanging out while she's here. But this isn't home for her. So—"

"The woman who owns The Mad Batter, right? Julia Prescott?"

I flung my wide eyes to hers, shocked she knew so much detail. "How—"

"I know everything going on with my kids." She placed her hand on my arm, her gesture comforting and filled with all the love she'd shown me since the day I was born. "And you, my dear boy, are one of my kids. Which is why I want the same for you as I do the rest of my children. To see you happy. It's what your mother would have wanted."

I sighed. "I know. It's just—"

My phone ringing pierced through the sound of easy conversation and forks scraping against plates as locals and tourists alike enjoyed *Eme*'s food. My stomach already growled from the myriad of incredible aromas surrounding me.

When I pulled my cell out of the pocket of my shorts

and saw my agent's name on the screen, a flicker of unease crossed my expression.

"It's important, yes?" *Eme* asked.

"My agent."

"Then answer. We'll talk later. Want a *loco moco?*"

I smiled. "You know I do."

"Good. I'll make you one."

"Thanks, *Eme.*"

"Anytime, Lochie."

Giving my hand a gentle squeeze, she retreated, continuing through the restaurant, stopping by each table, talking to every person as if they were family, even if they were complete strangers.

Returning my attention to my phone, I hit the answer button as I slipped out onto the back deck. The sun warmed my face, only a few clouds in the brilliant, blue sky. Despite it only being a little after nine, the shoreline already teemed with beachgoers determined to enjoy everything Hawaii had to offer.

"Hey, Brett."

"Good news, Lachlan!" he replied, exuding all the charm and charisma that convinced me to hire him as my agent. "Detective Walker is out of the hospital."

I didn't immediately respond, having momentarily forgotten what he was talking about. Truthfully, the events that led to me hopping on a flight to Hawaii hadn't exactly been at the forefront of my mind lately. The only thing that *had* been on my mind these past few days had been Julia. Not her past. Not my past. Just us. Just now.

Like we promised.

It was a reminder that, thousands of miles away, outside of the bubble we had made for ourselves, reality waited for me.

For us.

"How's he doing?" I asked, snapping out of my thoughts. "Any long-term...complications?"

"Nah. It apparently looked worse than it really was because of all the blood. He'll make a full recovery. Luckily for you, the DA has decided to *not* file charges. And Detective Walker has no intention of suing. Not sure why or what caused them to be so benevolent and understanding when they were adamant they wanted you to pay, but maybe they all realized the distress the situation caused you and decided to show some humanity. Doesn't matter why. But that's what they decided. So if I were you, I'd be thanking God, Allah, whomever you believe in, because someone up there has got your back."

"I sure will," I said, exhaling a long breath.

Granted, the possibility of criminal charges being filed hadn't exactly been on my radar, but it was still a relief to know, once I returned to Atlanta, I wouldn't have to deal with that on top of everything else.

"And please, I beg of you, don't pull a stunt like this in the future. I guarantee the next bastard you land in the hospital *will* sue you for everything you're worth. And then some."

"Duly noted. I will endeavor to refrain from breaking any more bones."

"Good. Now, there's still the issue with management."

"Management?" I furrowed my brows. "What issue is there? The cop isn't suing me. No charges are being filed. It's over."

"Not exactly. I just got off the phone with Buckley. They want to meet with you first thing Monday morning to discuss this incident."

"Monday?" I blinked, heart dropping to the pit of my stomach. "But I'm supposed to be on bereavement leave. I—"

"Do you honestly want me to tell the President of Baseball Operations for Atlanta that you can't make it because you're too busy surfing or sticking your dick in some tourist over there? I've had my ear to the ground, trying to see where their heads are. Buckley wants to make an example out of you. Suspend you for the rest of the season. You punched three cops. If I were in your shoes, I wouldn't question management right now. If they want you to show up at nine o'clock Monday morning, you show up. Don't act like a goddamn prima donna. Pretend like you actually give a shit and don't want to piss your career down the toilet. And, for God's sake, wear a fucking tie. Got it?"

I pushed out a long breath, running a hand over my face.

If I'd received this phone call a week ago, I would have happily jumped on a flight back to Atlanta without a second thought.

Hell, I would have welcomed the excuse to get off this island.

That was before.

Now, I hated the idea of leaving this place. Of bursting our bubble before it was time.

But if I had to be back in Atlanta Monday morning, I needed to leave Hawaii tomorrow.

The little time I had left with Julia was now down to less than a day.

"I'll be there," I finally said, voice filled with resignation.

"Great. See you then. And remember—"

"I got it. I'll wear a bloody tie."

Pulling my phone from my ear, I ended the call, shoving my cell back into my pocket, frustration tightening my muscles.

Closing my eyes, I drew in a deep breath, attempting to make sense of my warring emotions over the prospect of boarding a plane and leaving this place.

Leaving Julia.

After I lost Piper, I couldn't get away from this island quickly enough, the mere thought of being surrounded by all the memories and guilt too much for me.

Now, though, I'd give anything to have a little more time here.

To have a little more time with Julia.

"*Howzit*, bruh?"

I whirled around, meeting Nikko's concerned gaze and forcing a smile. "Hey, cousin."

Walking toward him, I grabbed the mug of coffee he held out and brought it to my lips. "Thanks, man."

"What did your agent want?" he pressed as we made our way toward an empty table. He pulled out a chair, lowering his imposing frame into it, eyes focused on me.

"The cops aren't filing charges," I replied as I sank into the chair across from him. "And that detective doesn't plan to sue me for damages, either. Probably because immediately after I was arrested, my agent made arrangements for me to cover all his medical bills."

"That's great." He beamed a relieved smile. Then his expression fell when mine didn't mirror his enthusiasm. He lifted a brow. "I assume there's more?"

I slowly nodded as *Eme* approached, two plates in her hands. Nikko jumped to his feet, striding toward her and taking the dishes.

"Thanks, *Eme*." Nikko pressed a kiss to his mother's cheek.

It was remarkable to think *Eme* gave birth to him. She was on the shorter side, with a little "meat" on her bones, as she liked to say. But her sons were enormous, all four of them over six feet tall with strong physiques. Regardless that they towered over her, she was still their mother. Still commanded their respect and admiration.

"Of course, my boy." She smiled and followed him to the table, assuming one of the empty chairs.

"So, what did your agent have to say?" she pressed before I had a chance to bite into her famous *loco moco*.

She even remembered the version I liked best — braised beef, instead of a hamburger patty, over white rice, smothered in gravy, a fried egg on top.

This most definitely was not part of my normal diet.

But since my hours on this island were now extremely limited, it was time to indulge in everything it had to offer.

I glanced across the table at Nikko, then *Eme*, figuring I may as well tell them both. *Eme* would find out anyway.

"Team management wants to meet with me to discuss my recent...actions."

"You mean when you punched that *lolo* detective because he wouldn't listen to you about Claire? If you ask me, he deserved what he got."

"Luckily, the police aren't going to file charges," I assured her, then glanced at Nikko. "But management still wants to talk to me." I paused. "Monday morning."

He blinked, the fork holding a generous bite of *loco moco* stopping halfway to his mouth. "But that means..."

I nodded sadly. "I have to leave tomorrow morning."

"Shit, bruh," he exhaled, leaning back in his chair, his breakfast now forgotten. "What are you going to do?"

"You mean about the girl?" *Eme* interjected.

"Yeah," I answered, not even trying to argue. "But there's not much I *can* do. We made an agreement to spend one week together while we were both in Hawaii. Since I leave tomorrow—"

"Do you have feelings for her?" *Eme* pressed before I could finish.

A part of me cursed Nikko for *Eme* finding out I'd been spending time with Julia. Then again, I'd always respected her advice. When my mother died, I often looked to her for guidance and reassurance I was on the right path.

I considered my response. *Did* I have feelings for Julia? I should feel awkward having this conversation with Nikko and *Eme*, considering they were Piper's family. I didn't, though. Not when they were now the only *ohana* I had left.

"It's...complicated," I said, using the same argument I'd made to myself and others all week.

"Well, simplify it for me," she instructed. "Take it down to the bare bones."

"The bare bones?"

"Yeah. The crux of it. What's stopping you from pursuing something with this girl?" She held up her hand when I opened my mouth to answer. "Other than some agreement to walk away, because that's not a good enough reason. Not for me. Not when I know how much you'll fight for something you truly want. So tell me what's preventing you from fighting for this."

I wasn't sure where to even begin, how much she knew. Then again, Nikko probably already told *Eme* everything we'd uncovered this week. How Caleb most likely hadn't been responsible for attacking Piper. That her assailant was still out there, harming more women.

"A lot. We're in two totally different places in our lives," I began, knowing I was taking the easy way out. "She's...a few years older."

"So?" She shrugged nonchalantly. "Your father was fifteen years older than your mother," she reminded me. "And they weren't simply in two totally different places in their lives. They were from two vastly different cultures." She hesitated, seeming to toil over her next words. "Did you know your grandparents didn't speak to your mother for five years after she moved to Melbourne and married your dad?"

I stopped the fork just short of my mouth, jaw dropping. "No. I..." I shook my head, this revelation hitting me hard.

I always thought my mum had a great relationship with my grandparents. At least that was how it seemed. They were some of the most loving people I'd ever been around. As were my mum and dad.

"I had no idea. Why?"

"This was over thirty years ago now. And your grandparents, well... They were from a slightly older generation. Your grandfather thought it better Lena marry someone familiar with our traditions. He worried she'd forget where she came from."

"But she never did," I argued. "All throughout my

childhood, even when we lived in Australia, she taught me her culture."

Eme reached across the table and placed her hand on mine. "I know that. It just took time for your grandfather to see it didn't matter where she was or how far she traveled. These islands and her people were always in her blood. Always a part of her.

"You see, your parents' relationship was complicated. There were a lot of reasons they could have walked away from each other. Settled for something easier. But that's exactly what they would have been doing. Settling for something less than what they deserved, probably regretting it the rest of their lives. Instead, they took a risk and made it work."

"How?" I asked, partly to learn about a side of my parents' relationship they'd never shared with me.

Partly because it gave me a sliver of hope that maybe Julia and I could follow the same path. Could overcome the obstacles facing us.

She squeezed my hand. "You may think you're from two different places. That you want two completely different things. Stop focusing on that. You need to find that place where you *do* connect. Where your lives *do* make sense together. That's where you'll find your strength. Where you'll find the magic. Everything else is just noise."

CHAPTER TWENTY-ONE

Julia

I couldn't get out of the car quickly enough, not even waiting for my driver to come around to open my door. All my obligations for the bakery were now officially behind me. For the next thirty-six hours, I could devote every second to Lachlan before I had to return to reality.

My heart squeezed at the notion that in just two days, I'd have to do precisely that. But I wasn't going to think about that. Not when we still had a little more time together.

And I planned on making the most out of every second.

After thanking the driver, I hurried up the walkway, rummaging through my purse for my keys. Finally finding them, I looked up, momentarily surprised when I saw

Lachlan sitting on the wicker chair by the front door, a suitcase by his side. Apparently he couldn't wait to see me, either. And he'd brought his things so he didn't have to go back to his place.

"You're early." I swayed my hips as I sauntered up, my pulse increasing as I took in his appearance. Black, button-down shirt, sleeves rolled up past his elbows. Khaki shorts. Flip-flops. And that sinful mouth turned up into a sly smile that had me remembering how much pleasure that mouth had given me.

"What can I say?" He stood. "The only thing I thought about all day was having yours lips on me again." He pressed a hand to my back and dragged my body against his as his mouth brushed mine.

I moaned into his kiss, doing everything in my power to ignore the fact that our kisses were numbered. Now wasn't the time to dwell on that. That wasn't how I wanted to spend our final few days. Instead, I wanted to pretend we were a normal couple who didn't have a time limit imposed on them.

A self-imposed time limit, but a time limit nonetheless.

Once he brought our kiss to an end, he took the keys from me and unlocked the door, helping steady me as I slipped off my shoes and left them in the basket in the foyer.

"Glass of wine?" I asked, glancing over my shoulder as I made my way into the kitchen.

"I'll get it."

Leaving his suitcase by the entryway, he walked toward the wine cabinet, carefully selecting a bottle. I leaned against the counter as I watched him. This entire scenario — walking through the door after a long day of work, picking out a wine, talking about what to have for dinner — was so domesticated. So...normal.

I liked it.

Wanted more of it.

But at what cost?

"Hope this is to your liking." Lachlan handed me the glass of red wine.

"Seeing as I bought all the wine, I'm pretty sure it'll pass muster." I winked.

He smiled, raising his glass. "To jellyfish."

My heart warmed at the memory of him making the same toast during our first date nearly a week ago. It felt like I was a completely different person back then.

I suppose I was. Lachlan changed me, encouraged me to take a chance. To put myself first.

For that, I'd always be grateful.

"I now have a renewed appreciation for those brainless bastards." I repeated the words he'd said that night.

"As do I." He clinked his glass against mine, eyes not straying from mine as we sipped on the robust red.

Then he lowered his glass and set it on the counter, clearing his throat. Instantly, I felt something shift. Like something was...off.

I couldn't explain it, but the air in the room grew unsettled. It could have simply been because our time together would soon be over.

But it felt deeper than that.

"Actually, there's another reason I decided to come by early."

I straightened, placing my glass beside his. "What's that?"

He gave me a half-hearted smile, as if trying to reassure me. But I couldn't fight the feeling I wasn't going to like what he was about to say.

Did Ethan find out more information? Something that strengthened the connection between my ex-husband and whomever was committing these recent crimes? Was there evidence Nick *was* involved, and not merely the inspiration of some other sociopath?

"My agent called."

"Oh." I smiled, somewhat relieved. But that relief vanished when Lachlan's expression grew even more morose.

It reminded me of the despair that oozed from every inch of him the night I saw him drunk on the beach and he revealed his sister was dead. Back when we were still strangers.

Now that I knew him, knew how he looked when he was happy, when he was angry, when he was frustrated, I knew whatever his agent had to say wasn't good.

I'd overheard rumblings about the possibility of a multi-game suspension. Had they made a decision? Seemed like shitty timing to me, especially considering he'd just lost his sister. I didn't think Lachlan was right in punching a cop, putting him in the hospital. But now I realized it came from a place of love for his sister. His *ohana*. After meeting some of his family, I knew he'd do anything for them.

Just like I got the feeling he'd do anything for me, too.

"He informed me management set up a meeting to discuss my little...incident. Apparently, putting a detective in the hospital is frowned upon by the powers that be." He laughed, but it wasn't natural. More nervous. Hesitant.

"And when is this meeting?" I asked, comforted by the fact they hadn't made a decision without allowing Lachlan the opportunity to explain himself.

At the same time, my unease increased. I doubted he'd feel the need to tell me about this unless it had something to do with me. With us. With the little time we had left.

He swallowed hard, his Adam's apple bobbing. "Nine o'clock Monday morning."

The words were like a punch to the gut, all the oxygen sucked from my body. Frustration built in my throat, making it hard to breathe, to think. I gripped the counter, needing it to steady myself when it felt like the world was spinning around me.

He ran a hand down my arm, attempting to soothe my unease, but I shook him off, pretending this sudden turn of events didn't affect me like it did.

"So you'll need to be back in Atlanta by then. And with the time difference and the length of the flight…"

"I need to leave tomorrow," he said solemnly. "My assistant arranged a charter for me at eight AM."

Pressure built in my chest, an ache unlike any I'd ever experienced filling me. My heart physically hurt at the reality that our remaining two days was now nothing more than a few hours.

"So this…" I dragged my gaze back up to his. "This is our last night together." My voice rose in pitch toward the end.

His shoulders fell as he pulled me into his arms. "I'm so sorry."

He dropped a kiss to my forehead, his embrace comforting, yet agonizing. A reminder that tomorrow at this time, these arms would be nothing but a distant memory.

"I tried to see if my agent could move the meeting, but I'm not exactly bargaining from a position of power here. He's of the mindset that if I don't want to face a lengthy suspension, I need to do whatever management asks. And they want me there at nine o'clock Monday morning."

I squeezed my eyes shut, pushing down every emotion fighting to rush to the surface. It was okay. What difference could a day or two make? Maybe it was better this way. Less time for him to steal another piece of my heart.

"I'm so sorry," he said again, his own voice choked. "But maybe—"

I pushed against him before he could finish his thought. "It's not a big deal." I flashed him a bright smile, averting my gaze. I couldn't, wouldn't look him in the eyes. If I did, I'd break.

And I couldn't break.

Not over this.

Not over something that wasn't supposed to mean anything.

Not over a week of sinful, lust-filled, depraved fucking.

Because that was all this was supposed to be. Nothing more. Nothing less.

Except it was so much more than that to me now.

And by the way he peered at me, I knew it was more to him, too.

"I was leaving on Monday anyway..." I continued chattering nervously. "So, really, we're only talking about a day. Plus, we both knew from the beginning this had an expiration date. So what if it's a day earlier?"

"Julia..." He exhaled, shaking his head. I could hear the apology in his tone. The concern. The unease.

The wish for something more.

Something that could never be.

"So, what shall we do tonight?" I asked, my voice bright and chipper as I rebuilt the wall around my heart, brick by heavy brick.

"Maybe dance the night away, get sloppy drunk on wine, then fuck until we pass out from exhaustion? I mean, if it's our last night together, we should probably go out with a bang. No pun intended. Or maybe the pun *is* intended."

My words came out fast and frenzied in an attempt to mask my heartbreak. Act as if this weren't the devastating news it was.

"Or would you rather—"

Before I could utter another syllable, his arms were around me, pulling me against his body, silencing my outburst. "I hate it, too," he murmured huskily, his voice pained. "I hate it, too."

My hands formed into fists as I fought to keep the tears at bay. I wasn't supposed to cry over this. Over some twenty-seven-year-old I had no business being with.

I shook my head, thinking that would help. That if I simply denied how much this upset me, it would all go away. That my heart wouldn't feel like it was shattering into a million pieces right now.

But when he tightened his hold on me, his arms achingly perfect as they gave me all the solace and acceptance I'd yearned for my entire life, a fissure formed in my heart, allowing everything to seep out.

"Damn you," I choked out through the ache in my throat, bringing my fists against his chest as I succumbed to my feelings. "*Goddamn you.*"

Cupping my face, he forced my gaze to his, not allowing me to hide from him, even though that was exactly what I wanted to do. His eyes were glossy with his own unshed tears, making it more than apparent this was just as difficult for him.

I peered deep into those azure pools that once were a mystery but had quickly become my solace. My sanctuary. He parted his lips, searching my gaze, his own warring thoughts etched in the hard ridges of his face. I felt his indecision. His confusion. His fear.

My breathing increased as I waited for his next words.

Instead, he crashed his lips against mine, kissing me in a way he never had before.

In a way I feared I'd never be kissed again.

He clung to me as his tongue coaxed my mouth open, treating me to one of my last tastes of this man.

This mysterious, infuriating, incredible man.

"Lachlan," I panted when he tore his lips from mine.

He pinched my chin, tilting my head back.

I brought my hand to his face, savoring in the roughness of his unshaven jawline against my skin. My heart hammered in my chest at the intensity with which he gazed upon me.

Would I ever have that again?

I couldn't be sure.

All I did know was that I didn't want to waste a second of the time we had left. I wanted to experience him in every way possible. In all the ways that had scared me.

Until now.

"I need you to make love to me."

His eyes searched mine for a moment, words seeming to escape him.

Then he covered my lips once more, stealing my breath.

And my heart.

CHAPTER TWENTY-TWO

Lachlan

I gripped her face, holding her tighter than I ever had as my tongue swept against hers, pouring everything into this kiss. There was so much I wanted to say. So much I wanted to thank her for.

So many reasons I *didn't* want this to end.

I just didn't know if it was enough.

Eme's words from earlier filtered into my subconsciousness, encouraging me to just tune out the noise and find our magic. And there was no question in my mind... This thing between us *was* magic.

"Julia," I began after bringing our kiss to an end, gaze focused intently on her. "What if—"

"Don't," she begged, as if able to sense what I was about

to say. "Please. Don't make this any more difficult. I guarantee you won't like my answer to what you're about to ask. This week hasn't changed my position on that matter. Nothing can. So let's just enjoy our last night in our bubble. Because this can't last outside of this bubble." A tear slid down her cheek, her words drenched in sadness. "Okay?"

I opened my mouth, on the verge of telling her all the reasons she was wrong. But I didn't want to spend what little time we had left arguing. Didn't want her to push me away before our time was over.

So instead, I reluctantly nodded. "Okay."

Lowering my mouth back to hers, I sealed my vow with a kiss. As I traced my hands down her body, I imprinted every delicious curve to memory, pretending the idea of never again feeling her in my arms wasn't the soul-crushing ending it was.

"Hold on tight," I murmured against her lips.

She only had seconds to react before I swooped her up into my arms in a cradle hold, carrying her from the kitchen and up the stairs. Her eyes remained locked on mine, glossy with emotion.

After crossing the threshold into the bedroom, I slowly lowered her to her feet, the atmosphere charged with a thousand emotions I was scared to label.

That neither one of us would.

If we did, it would be too painful. Too real.

And this was never supposed to be real.

I touched my lips to hers, sighing into her perfect kiss. I'd always thought her kisses addictive, even more so once we dropped the pretenses and shared our true selves with each other.

But this one was so much more charged.

So much more vibrant.

So much more electrifying.

I looped an arm around her waist, her body flush with mine. So warm. So inviting. So damn perfect. It was as if our lips were made to do just this. Our hearts made to beat for each other. Our souls destined to be inexplicably intertwined for all eternity.

I felt it that first night I touched my forehead to hers.

And I still felt it.

My hands on her hips, I backed her the few steps toward the bed, my lips never leaving hers.

"I need you," she begged against my mouth as she attempted to yank off my shirt. "Need to feel you. Need you inside me."

"Then that's what you shall have."

I stepped back, reaching for the top button of my shirt.

"Let me," she murmured seductively.

Her emerald eyes no longer awash with heartache but desire, she unbuttoned my shirt with slow, languid motions, each second ratcheting up my need for her even more. I wanted to tear my clothes from my body. Hers, too.

But that wasn't what this was. Not to me.

She wanted me to make love to her. That was precisely what I planned to do.

When she undid the final button, she pushed my shirt down my arms, allowing it to fall into a heap on the floor. She paused for a moment to take in my appearance, her skin flushed with appreciation.

As she reached for my belt and unbuckled it, I didn't take my eyes off her, the air between us sizzling with sexual tension.

Once she pushed my shorts and briefs down my legs, I stepped out of them, smiling slyly when I noticed her attention immediately go to my erection.

"God bless Australia," she exhaled, much like she did our first night together. This time, though, there was a hint of sadness in her words.

"My turn." I touched a hand to her hip and turned her around.

With deliberate motions, I lowered the zipper of her dress and pushed the sleeves off her shoulders, the fabric pooling at her feet. I helped her step out of it before unhooking her bra, dropping it to the floor.

Turning her to face me, I took in her body, my arousal hardening in appreciation of every curve, every valley.

Days ago, she'd attempted to hide from me, nervous and apprehensive about me seeing her naked.

Not anymore.

We'd stripped each other of more than just our clothes. We bore our souls to each other. Exposed our truths.

Dropping to my knees, I peppered kisses along her stomach. As I slid her panties down her legs, my mouth moving past her belly button and toward her hips, her breathing increased.

When I trailed a finger up her thighs, she parted her legs in invitation, a whimper falling from her throat as I brushed against her center, spreading her need for me around.

"Oh god..." She ran her hands through my hair, tugging and pulling, as if it were the only thing that could keep her grounded.

"I need to taste you," I said. "Need to have you."

"I'm yours," she exhaled.

"Mine." I stood and laid her down on the bed, then lowered myself on top of her.

I covered her mouth with mine, desperate to lose myself in her kiss, her taste, her everything before I had no choice but to come back up for air in a matter of hours. Moving from her lips, I left kisses along her jawline before shifting to her neck and collarbone.

I snaked down her frame, her chest heaving with every nip, every suck, every lick as I worshipped her in the way she needed. In the way she deserved.

When I settled between her thighs, I glanced up at her, a smirk crawling across my lips as I teased her folds.

"Long live the South." I waggled my brows.

She brought her gaze to mine, sadness consuming her, but she tried to smile through it. Just as I supposed she had most of her life. Masked her emotions with a smile. But she couldn't hide them from me. Not anymore. I saw all of her. And for that, for allowing me to see the real Julia, I'd be forever grateful.

Smoothing my hands down her stomach, I flicked my tongue along her clit, her body moving against mine as I feasted on her, savoring the way she tasted. The way she felt. The way she hummed in appreciation.

God, she was so damn responsive to each brush of my tongue or swipe of my fingers as I explored every inch of her. When her breaths became sharper and more uneven, her movements more ragged, I knew she was close.

But, in typical Julia fashion, she fought it.

I wasn't going to let her.

Not tonight.

Not when this was one of our last times together.

"Let go, Julia. Just let yourself go."

I increased my motions, gently nibbling on her clit as I inserted another finger, hitting that spot inside her I knew drove her wild.

She screamed out, body quivering and trembling as her orgasm overtook her. I continued torturing her with my tongue and fingers, not wanting her to ever come down. Wanting her to stay in the clouds with me forever.

When her shivers began to wane, I inched back up her body. Her lips were on mine in an instant, her kiss searing every inch of me with need.

Pulling back to meet her eyes, I stroked my erection, bringing it up to her center.

"This isn't just sex for me, Julia," I murmured, wanting her to see the truth in my words. To *feel* the truth in my words. She may not have wanted to hear this...for me to make a final stand, so to speak...but she deserved to know. "It never has been."

I held her gaze, her lips parting, a response seemingly on the tip of her tongue.

But, as always, she refused to voice her feelings, suppressing them instead.

"Let me feel you," she begged, fingers digging into my back.

Groaning at her achingly perfect touch, I slowly pushed into her, her eyes rolling into the back of her head, expression one of pure bliss.

I covered her lips with mine as I moved inside her, wordlessly trying to show her with my deliberate, gentle rhythm how much she meant to me. How much I admired her.

How much I needed her.

"Look at me, Julia," I demanded.

She snapped her eyes to mine, the green hue dark with want.

"Stay with me," I murmured, needing the reminder that she was still here with me, even if it was fleeting.

"I'm here. I'm with you."

"Oh god," I exhaled, the feeling of her around me almost more than I could handle.

I buried my face in her neck, sucking and kissing as I rocked my hips against her. This wasn't the relentless fucking that had been our norm only a few days ago. Hell, only a few hours ago. This was different in every way possible.

Because this was goodbye.

I crashed my lips against hers, my thrusts becoming more determined, yet still filled with the veneration she deserved.

She wrapped her legs around my waist, fingers threading through my hair. "Fall with me," she murmured.

Her words were my undoing, pushing me over the edge as she clenched around me. I drove into her, unable to stop feeling her, savoring her, worshipping her, until I stilled. Letting out a strangled cry that was a combination of euphoria and despair, I jerked through my release at the same time as she rode out her own orgasm in one incredible moment of bliss.

Our ragged breathing echoed in the room as we remained a mess of arms and legs, neither of us wanting to pull away. Not wanting this moment to end.

Not wanting *us* to end.

But there never was an us.

And there never would be.

Once my heart rate returned to somewhat normal, my lungs able to capture enough air, I met her gaze, silent tears sliding down her cheeks. I offered her a sad smile, fighting against my own emotions.

Gradually bringing my forehead to hers, I closed my eyes as we connected *alo* to *alo*.

Soul to soul.

Heart to heart.

One last time.

CHAPTER TWENTY-THREE

Julia

The tickle of the ocean breeze against my skin stirred me awake, seagulls squawking in the distance cutting through the haze of a hard-fought few hours' sleep. I hadn't wanted to fall asleep in the first place, both Lachlan and I doing everything to resist succumbing to our body's needs, not wanting to waste a second of what little time we had together with something as unimportant as sleep.

But we were powerless to resist.

Now, I didn't want to open my eyes for fear I would be met with the brilliant sun streaming into the bedroom, a reminder that it was day.

And the hours we had left were now down to mere minutes.

As if sensing my brain stirring, Lachlan snaked an arm around my waist, pulling my body flush with his, my back to his front. He left a trail of kisses along my shoulder blades, and I sighed into his touch.

"Whatever you do, don't open your eyes, love," he crooned, his voice husky from sleep.

"Why?"

"Because that bastard sun has made a rather unwelcome appearance."

"It couldn't be. It's far too early. It must be the moon."

On a long sigh, he tightened his embrace, as if by doing so, it would make my statement true. "You're right. It's the moon."

I turned over in bed, meeting his gaze. "See?" I smiled sadly, a tear sliding down my cheek. "It's still night. We still have time."

He drew in a quivering breath. "We still have time."

He crushed his mouth to mine, desperation and heartache dripping from every inch of him as he kissed me for one of the last times.

My heart physically ached at the reminder I'd have to go to sleep all alone tonight. That I'd wake up all alone tomorrow. Then have breakfast all alone. It had only been a week, but in that time, this man had become such a huge part of my everyday life. At least here on Hawaii.

A voice inside me reminded me he could be a part of my life in Atlanta, too, if I would finally take a risk.

But like I'd cautioned myself repeatedly over the past

few days, and especially last night as Lachlan and I spent hours exploring his Hawaii, everything about it making me feel like we were a real couple, I didn't have a choice. I had too much to lose.

Deepening the kiss in the hopes of drowning out that voice, I pushed him onto his back. I circled my hips against his erection, the feeling of him teasing and tempting in all the ways I'd grown accustomed.

I pulled away, eyes locking with his as he brought his arousal up to me.

He arched a brow. "One last time?"

I nodded, swallowing past the painful lump in my throat. "One last time," I managed to say.

He slowly eased inside me, filling me in the way only he could. In a way I doubted anyone ever would again.

Neither one of us said a word as I moved against him. We didn't need to. Words had become inconsequential and unnecessary between us. Instead, we communicated the way we had all week. With our bodies. Our hearts. Our souls.

"Remember me," he begged, his words puncturing my heart. He cupped my cheek, his hold unwavering, powerful.

I covered his hand with mine, not wanting to let go for fear this would all be over. But it had to end.

It *had* to.

"I'll never forget," I promised, lowering my lips back to his. "I'll never forget."

"Julia," he exhaled, his words a mix between a moan and a cry. A rare moment of vulnerability for a man who, a week ago, masked his feelings with anger and resentment. Now, he happily exposed his emotions for me to see.

To allow me to possess the parts of him no one ever had.

Just as I'd allowed him to possess the pieces of me I'd refused to give anybody else. The pieces of myself I didn't think existed. The pieces of myself I thought Nick had killed ages ago.

But he hadn't. I just needed the right person to bring them out again. To give them life once more.

Breaths increasing, my motions became more frenzied as I chased that sensation I'd grown to crave. At the same time, I fought it, not wanting this to be over so soon, struggling to draw it out as long as possible.

But when Lachlan pressed his thumb to my clit and rubbed it in that achingly perfect way he knew I hungered for, I could no longer fight this carnal need for release and satisfaction, my body a slave to his touch.

When his lips captured mine, his tongue teasing mine was the last straw. I fell apart around him just as he released a strangled cry, giving in to one last moment of bliss.

Of euphoria.

Of happiness.

CHAPTER TWENTY-FOUR

Lachlan

I rolled my suitcase toward the foyer and peeked out one of the windows, spying a black SUV waiting to take me to the airport. It was an ominous sight, a reminder that this really was the end. That I was supposed to board that plane and forget this past week ever happened.

But I never would.

I'd always remember Julia. Even if she wanted nothing more than to forget me.

"Your ride's here," she stated, voice catching.

Exhaling a long breath, I turned to face her. Thankfully I'd brought my things with me yesterday so I could leave straight from here, instead of wasting the preciously little time we had together this morning to head to my mum's house to pack.

"Yeah." I smiled sadly. "My charter leaves in about forty-five minutes, so I should probably get going."

"At least you don't have to worry about getting to the airport two hours before your flight like you do when flying commercial." She pushed out a nervous laugh.

"Thank goodness for small miracles."

I swept my gaze over her, unsure what to say. How to even begin to say goodbye. There was so much I wanted to tell her. How much I admired her. Cared for her. Appreciated her.

But instead of filling our last few seconds with words, I cupped her cheeks and pressed my lips to hers, hungry for one last taste of her.

The finality of this moment overtaking her, she flung her arms around my neck, kissing me with urgency, with need, with unrelenting desperation as we relished in what we'd become to each other.

It was hard to believe we'd first crossed paths merely a week ago. She'd fallen on the beach after stepping on a jellyfish. I wanted nothing to do with anyone or anything, content to wallow in my own anger and self-loathing.

Despite that, neither of us could fight the attraction from that first chance meeting. And every day afterward, I couldn't shake the feeling there was a reason her path crossed mine.

Now I know with certainty what the reason was. To give me the answers I'd needed for years. To give me peace.

To give me understanding.

The sound of a *ping* cut through the exchange, most likely a text from my driver telling me he was out front.

I sighed, bringing our kiss to an end, although it was the last thing I wanted. I wanted to stay in this bubble with Julia. But that wasn't our reality.

Julia placed her hands on my chest, keeping her eyes averted. "You need to go."

"I do."

I tightened my embrace, wishing I could keep her here forever. I hated the idea of letting her go. Of never feeling her body against mine again.

"Thank you," I murmured against her head.

"For what? Letting you screw me all week?" She laughed nervously, as she always did whenever she felt anxious.

Just one of the many things I'd learned about her this week.

"No." Grasping her chin, I forced her eyes to mine. "For teaching me how to forgive myself." I rested my forehead against hers. "For that, I will *never* forget you, Julia."

She choked out a sob, her body trembling as she fought against her tears. "I'll never forget you, either, Lachlan."

I covered her mouth with mine once more, our tongues tangling as we poured everything we felt into one last kiss.

One last heartbeat.

One last goodbye.

When my phone *pinged* again, I cursed the driver for bursting our bubble before I was ready. I doubted I'd ever truly be ready, though. Not after everything we'd shared this week.

Meeting her eyes, I held her gaze for several moments. Then I reluctantly released her and turned, walking away from the best thing to ever happen to me. Every step I took was a struggle, like my body had to physically fight my heart in order to put one foot in front of the other.

I pulled the door open, the thick, summer air assaulting me. Grasping the handle of my suitcase, I was about to step outside when I stopped. I squeezed my eyes shut, pinching the bridge of my nose as thousands of thoughts and emotions warred within me.

"Did you forget something?" Julia asked.

"Did I forget something?" I shook my head, laughing slightly at the irony in her question. "You know what? I absolutely *did* forget something."

Whirling around, I advanced on her, framing her face in my hands so she couldn't escape the conversation she didn't want to have last night.

"What are you—"

"I swore I wouldn't do this," I interrupted, needing to get it off my chest before I lost my nerve. Before I convinced myself it was a bad idea. "That I wouldn't like your answer. But that was last night. When we still had time. Something we no longer have. So right now, I have absolutely nothing to lose... Except the one thing I can't stomach living without."

"And what's that?" she asked in a shaky voice.

"You."

She released a tiny breath, eyes filling with tears as my admission echoed around us, time seeming to stretch.

"I've been trying to tell myself I was crazy for even considering this because of how different our lives are," I continued when she didn't immediately respond. "But the truth is, I want to be with you. With the quirky woman who wears t-shirts with somewhat inappropriate sayings on them. With the sexy woman who makes my heart beat faster than it has in years. With the badass woman who's endured more horror than any human should ever have to, yet somehow still manages to smile. And make other people smile, too. You made *me* smile again."

She shook her head, wiping at the tears now falling steadily down her face, still seemingly in denial about this. About us.

"I get it." I moved my hands to her biceps, holding her tightly. "I know I promised I'd walk away. But I don't want to. I can't. I want you in my life. Want to wake up in the morning and bury my head in your hair. Want to cook you breakfast. Want to rub your feet. Want to laugh with you. Get angry with you.

"I don't care *what* we do. We could spend hours walking up and down the aisles of the bloody farmer's market. It doesn't matter. I just..."

I licked my lips, peering intently into her eyes. Then I brought a hand to her cheek. She closed her eyes, melting into the contact.

I curved toward her, my lips a breath from hers. "I just want to be with you, Julia. Nothing more. Nothing less," I murmured, allowing my confession to sink in.

A confession I honestly thought I'd leave this island without telling her.

But *Eme* was right. The past twelve hours solidified that. There was a lot of noise in both our lives, but when we tuned it out, like we did in this bubble we'd created for ourselves, it was fucking magical.

I wanted more of it.

Hell, I wanted *all* of it.

"Lachlan..." Julia lifted her gaze to mine, sorrow and remorse covering every inch of her. I could practically taste her rejection.

"I know it's crazy." I dropped my hold, pacing in front of her. "Trust me. I *know*. There are dozens of reasons this would never work out. I've gone over every single one of them. We're in two totally different places in our lives. You're worried about your ex, and for good reason. You have a teenage daughter who may or may not understand why her mum's seeing someone who's so much younger. I'm pretty sure the age difference between us is the same as it is between your daughter and me."

Julia laughed through her tears. "If you're trying to make a strong case for yourself, I'm not sure that's the best way to do it."

"That may be true..." I approached her again, holding her cheeks tightly in my hands. "But I want you to know right here, right now, I don't care about any of that. About the dozens of reasons you could come up with about why this is a horrible fucking idea. The only thing I care about is *you*. I want to be with *you*, to hell with the risk. Your ex-husband doesn't scare me. Not like the idea of losing you does. Never feeling your lips on mine again, your skin on mine, your heart beat in time with mine... That is goddamn petrifying, Julia. *That's* what scares me."

She blinked, mouth agape as she attempted to process everything. Waves crashed in the distance, intermingling with the occasional squealing child on the beach and ticking of the clock in the living room.

A reminder that our time was fleeting.

"I don't... I don't know what to say," she finally responded.

"I don't want you to say anything. Not here. Not now. I don't think this is a decision you're able to make right now. I can absolutely appreciate the fact this is a bigger deal for you than it is for me. That you have a lot more to think about before making such a big decision. I don't expect you to throw caution to the wind and jump into this without giving it careful deliberation."

I looped an arm around her waist, pulling her body against mine. "But after that careful deliberation, I'd really like it if you could find it in your heart to choose me over fear. Can you promise me that? That you'll think about it?" I arched a brow, bracing myself for her refusal.

To my surprise, she nodded. "Okay."

Relief enveloped me in response to that single word. One that was uttered hundreds, even thousands of times a day.

But that one word filled me with more hope than I'd experienced in a long time.

Maybe ever.

"Okay," I repeated, gradually lowering my lips to hers.

"Okay," she said once more, moving her mouth against mine in what I prayed wouldn't be our last kiss.

CHAPTER TWENTY-FIVE

Lachlan

Voices argued around me as I sat in the conference room in the sky deck of the ballpark, everyone discussing my behavior as if I weren't even here. As if I were inconsequential. A piece of property.

That was probably all I was to them. A piece of property to be traded when I started giving them too many problems.

On our way here, Brett told me to stay quiet and let him do all the talking. I wasn't going to argue with that. I was more than aware of my tendency to run my mouth when angry.

And I should have been furious.

But I wasn't.

I knew the President of Baseball Operations, Clark

Buckley, had tossed around the possibility of a multi-game suspension. To hear him propose leaving me off the roster for the remainder of the year should have felt like a knife to the chest, considering my age.

Sure, I was only twenty-seven. But the average retirement age for baseball players is around twenty-nine or thirty. There are definitely exceptions to the rule. Hell, Curt Schilling pitched the Red Sox to their first World Series title in eighty-six years when he was in his forties.

But that wasn't the norm, especially for a pitcher, who puts excess strain on his body above and beyond the average player. So to sit here and remain silent while the team managers debated suspending me for the rest of the season should have gutted me, considering all the sacrifices I'd made to get to where I was.

Yet it didn't. Not like it should have.

Because I'd finally found something that mattered more to me than any short-lived baseball career.

I just prayed Julia would eventually come to realize that.

I didn't even want to consider any other possibility.

Every minute I didn't hear from her caused me to lose more and more hope. It didn't matter it was only Monday morning, that she was presumably still on the island. I hated not knowing. I wanted to do the right thing. Give her time to sort it out in her head.

But how long would I have to wait?

A day?

A week?

A year?

Forever?

"You can't be serious, Clark!" Brett's voice cut through, snapping me out of my thoughts.

He'd spent the last half-hour arguing on my behalf, pointing out that not only was I under extreme emotional distress at the time of the assault, but that I'd also already made a hefty donation to the Fallen Officers Foundation, as well as took care of Detective Walker's medical bills.

That didn't seem to matter to the management team, though. At least not Clark Buckley. As the President of Operations, he was essentially the middleman between the team managers and the owners, making all the important decisions regarding the roster.

Including any regarding disciplinary actions.

As much as the team managers might come to my defense, at the end of the day, Clark Buckley had the last word.

And I feared I wasn't going to like what that last word was.

"This was a little altercation. One Mr. Hale has already publicly apologized for, as well as made amends to the victim. The DA decided not to press charges, yet you want to punish him by benching him the remainder of the season? That's a bit extreme."

"This wasn't just a simple bar brawl with minimal injuries," Clark said evenly, keeping his shoulders square, spine straight. His thinning, gray hair was plastered to his head, but no amount of product in the world could make up for the hair loss that had grown more and more prominent the past several years. "He assaulted three law enforcement officers. They may have opted to not press charges for whatever reason, but several years ago, this organization decided to take a hard line when it came to players being involved in any sort of violence, particularly altercations with law enforcement. Need I remind you our club hasn't had the best history when it comes to players respecting the police. A tough suspension sends a very clear message that we won't condone this kind of behavior."

"I absolutely agree with you," Brett said. "And I applaud the measures management has taken in this regard, considering domestic violence tends to be an issue among some."

"Precisely why we need to take a hard stance here. Why—"

"Mr. Buckley, if I may offer *my* opinion," Daxton Shea said from the far end of the long table, speaking up for the first time since this meeting began.

Clark raised a single brow, his proverbial feathers seemingly ruffled over the idea of having to listen to Daxton...or Dax, as he preferred to be called...considering he was only twenty-seven. But he didn't have a choice. Clark Buckley may have been President of Operations, but Daxton was one of the owners, here to represent not only *his* interests, but also his parents', who owned the remaining interests in the team. As such, he could fire anyone here.

Including Clark.

"We're always more than happy to take your position into account," Clark said with a fabricated smile.

"Wonderful."

He stood, resecuring the button on his jacket, everything about him exuding wealth and class. His suit probably cost more than most people made in a month. His blond hair was slicked back. Even his nails were neatly manicured.

I was one of the highest paid pitchers in the history of professional baseball. But my five-year contract for $100 million was peanuts compared to the billions of dollars Dax's family was worth.

"As part of the management team, your job is to look at numbers and make a decision based on the empirical data," Dax began, leisurely walking around the table. "Earned run average. Batting average. On-base percentage. Slugging percentage. On-base *plus* slugging percentage. You've got notebooks upon notebooks filled with this information. All black and white. No gray area." He stopped walking, addressing Clark directly. "Believe me, I hate the gray area, too. But life isn't so simple, I'm afraid."

He began pacing again, an air of authority about him as he spoke to this group of men who easily had at least ten or fifteen years on him.

"I may be young, but I know we've all made our fair

share of mistakes we regret. That we'd do anything to take back."

He stopped in front of James Baker, the team's general manager. "Didn't you start an on-field brawl that resulted in only a small fine, even after breaking an umpire's nose?"

"I was having a bad day behind the plate," he explained remorsefully. "Let too many balls get past me."

"And on that day you let too many balls get past you, had you just...I don't know...experienced a loved one's sudden and unexpected death?"

"No, I hadn't." Baker lifted his gaze to mine again, a silent apology within.

I gave him an appreciative smile, a glimmer of hope filling me that maybe there was some sort of light at the end of the tunnel. That I wasn't on the brink of kissing the rest of the season, possibly my career, goodbye.

"How about you, Aaron?" Dax walked behind the table, patting our first base coach's back. "You took a curveball in the knee and stormed the mound, landing the pitcher in the hospital for a week. And, if I recall correctly, that pitcher retired the next year."

Aaron nodded solemnly. "He retired because of long-term effects of the injuries he suffered as a result of the fight. I've never forgiven myself for that."

"Were you suspended for any games?"

"No."

Dax grinned, satisfied that his point was finally coming across. "I didn't think so."

He shifted his focus to Clark. "And how about you, Mr. Buckley. You were once a player yourself. A left-handed pitcher with a hell of a curveball, just like Mr. Hale here. I seem to remember you punched your coach after he took you out of the game because you'd given up too many runs. Does that ring a bell?"

Clark squeezed his eyes shut. "It does."

"If my research is on point, and it usually is, your coach required reconstructive surgery on his jaw. Correct?"

He reluctantly nodded.

"And how many games were you suspended for?" Dax pressed.

Clark hung his head. "None," he answered softly.

"I'm sorry." Dax put his hand up to his ear, pretending he couldn't hear. "How many?"

"Zero," Clark said, louder this time.

"Exactly."

He looked around the table, gaze stopping on each man. "Every one of you has been in some sort of scuffle. Some sort of fight that caused injury to another. But you were never suspended for a single game. And you only lashed out because your ego got the better of you. That's not the case here."

Dax moved to my side of the table, placing his hands on my shoulders.

"Mr. Hale acted the way he did out of distress. He'd just lost his sister. Was called down to identify her body. Have any of you ever received a phone call in the middle of the night informing you your only family was dead? That you were needed to confirm that, yes, the cold corpse lying on that metal table was someone you love?"

I swallowed hard, pushing down the renewed emotion at the reminder of that night, the guilt still as strong as it was when I received that phone call.

"So while I certainly don't condone his behavior, I think we can all appreciate his actions weren't completely intentional. Were the result of emotional distress after losing his sister, whom we all know he was extremely close to."

With each word he spoke, Dax's voice grew louder and more assured, exuding the image of a man in control. A person of authority.

I wasn't entirely sure *why* he felt the need to defend my actions when the owners typically didn't care what team management did, as long as the seats were filled each game. Not to mention, suspending me without pay would save them a small fortune. But I wouldn't question it. Not if it meant I could still play ball. I feared that would be the only thing to help take my mind off Julia.

"We've all made mistakes. And we've all had reasons for making those mistakes. Not excuses. *Reasons*. Lachlan has suffered immense loss since he signed on with this club. First, his girlfriend, mere days after he was finally promoted to the majors. And just a little over a week ago, his sister. Now, let me ask all of you... Do you think you'd make the best decisions after losing someone you loved dearly? I know I wouldn't."

Silence filled the room as the management team looked at each other, none of them arguing Dax's point. Brett caught my eye and gave me a slight smile that was a mixture of relief and excitement.

"I get that I'm just an owner. Just the money. That we're not given all the information and are supposed to leave the decisions regarding players to you, our well-qualified management team. But I speak for a great many people, fans and players alike, who feel that any lengthy suspension would be too harsh a punishment, especially after everything Lachlan's already lost. We should show him compassion. After all, we're supposed to be family. Family doesn't turn its back on each other. It's supposed to support each other. So I implore you. Let's support Lachlan. Not punish him."

A thick tension permeated the room as I stared ahead, awaiting Buckley's determination. He no longer wore a self-satisfied smirk, but I still wasn't sure where his head was. If he planned to stick to his initial proposal of a season-long suspension simply because he could, regardless of Dax Shea's argument.

"I suppose I *may* have proposed a punishment that could be considered a bit extreme, especially under the circumstances," Buckley finally said. He glanced down at the papers in front of him before looking back at me, brow raised. "You've paid all the detective's medical bills?"

I opened my mouth to answer, but Brett spoke over me.

"Yes. And he's agreed to cover any rehabilitation therapy that may be needed."

Buckley nodded. Then he pushed out a deep breath. "I can appreciate how distressing the situation must have been for you. Grief makes us all act in ways we may not be able to control. So, this time, I'll heed the advice of the other men in this room and not impose a suspension on you."

Brett exhaled, relieved, placing his hand on my shoulder and squeezing.

I turned to him, forcing out a smile, since he probably expected some sort of reaction to the news I wouldn't be sitting out the remainder of the season.

"But if you act out like this again, I can assure you, the outcome will be vastly different," Clark admonished.

"He won't. I'll make sure of it," Brett responded.

I should have been thrilled. This was my career.

My life's ambitions.

The only dream I ever had.

The only thing that ever mattered to me.

Until now…

I glanced out the windows, looking at the pristine, green grass of the baseball field, the Atlanta skyline visible in the distance.

A week ago, this was the only place that felt even remotely like home to me. The smell of fresh-cut grass, leather, and something unique to baseball stadiums usually filled me with peace and excitement.

Now I longed for the scent of lavender, vanilla, and hummingbird cake.

I just prayed yesterday wasn't the last time I'd ever experience it.

CHAPTER TWENTY-SIX

Julia

"Home sweet home," Naomi remarked as she helped me carry my bags up to my house in the Atlanta suburb of Brookhaven that I'd bought after my former life fell apart.

It made sense to start over again here. After all, my brother lived right down the street. Throughout my life, he'd been one of the few people I could always count on to have my back, no matter what. And that still held true.

"Thanks for giving me a ride home."

"It's the least I could do after you treated me to a week in Hawaii."

"It was a work trip," I reminded her.

"Sure it was." She winked. "Plus, I knew I could finally

get you to spill the tea about how you and Lachlan left things."

"Always an ulterior motive with you." I rolled my eyes, feigning annoyance. But I could never be annoyed with Naomi.

Despite everything I'd been through this past week... hell, these past few years...she always had my back. Always supported me, no questions asked.

Everyone needed a friend like Naomi in their lives.

Which was why, during the drive from the airport to my place, I didn't think twice about sharing Lachlan's heartfelt plea with her. It was probably a good thing she waited until we were alone to push me for information, because talking about it opened the flood gates again, my tears relentless as I relayed his passionate words.

But they really weren't tears of sadness.

They were more like tears of joy. Like my heart was so full of emotion from the way he felt about me that it could no longer keep it all in.

"I may have an ulterior motive, but it comes from a place of love." She wrapped me in her arms, squeezing tightly.

"I know." I returned her hug, finding strength in my best friend's encouraging embrace.

"And I am so dang proud of you for how you handled this week."

"You're proud of me?" I pulled back. "For what? Spreading my legs and getting laid?"

"No...," she drew out. "Well, kind of. But I'm more proud of you for taking a risk and finally making yourself a priority for the first time in, well...your entire life." She gave me a reassuring smile, then looked into the distance, seemingly deep in thought.

"What is it?" I pressed.

"It's funny." She brought her gaze back to mine. "I never understood the saying before. Thought it was some bullshit motivational thing greeting card companies made up. But now... I get it."

"Get what?" I peered at her quizzically, brows scrunched.

"That lame saying that used to make me want to gag. *'Don't cry because it's over. Smile because it happened.'* That's what I'm doing. I'm beaming because something good finally happened to you, Jules. Something you deserve. Hopefully your week of sinful, lust-filled, depraved fucking was merely the first chapter in a book filled with lots and lots of happy endings..." She waggled her brows. "If you know what I mean."

I studied her for a beat, then burst out laughing, the wide range of emotions I'd experienced the past few days spilling forward.

"Only you can turn a meaningful moment into something sick and disturbing."

"It's a gift," she acknowledged, wrapping her arms around me again. "A rare and valuable gift."

I sighed. "That it is."

"I may joke around a lot," she continued, her voice turning serious as she rubbed my back, "but I mean it. I *am* proud of you."

"And here I thought you'd be mad I didn't jump at Lachlan's offer, considering you were the one who practically begged me to sleep with him."

She released me and raised a finger. "Okay, first of all, there was no 'practically'. I *did* beg you to fuck him. You needed a good lay. Worse than anyone in the history of sex."

There was a time I would have shied away from this conversation, reminded her I was her boss and we shouldn't talk about sex. But I hadn't acted like her boss in years. Sure, she worked for me, but she'd always been more of a friend.

And now, family.

"And second of all," she continued, dropping her hand to her side, sarcastic expression falling, "you made the right decision, Jules."

"I did?"

This certainly took me by surprise, especially considering all her pep talks about putting myself first.

"Yes. And Lachlan was smart enough to know you weren't in the right place to make a decision, either. How could you decide what you truly wanted when you were in some strange, tropical paradise limbo? Hawaii's Lachlan's home. Not yours. You couldn't make any sort of decision about him until you were here." She waved her hand at my house. "You needed to come down from the clouds to decide if you wanted to fly again." She pulled me in for one last hug. "And I really hope you decide to fly again."

I closed my eyes, relishing in her embrace.

Being back here, surrounded by all the memories of my past and why things had to be the way they were, should have solidified my original position about why I couldn't pursue anything with Lachlan.

But it didn't.

It only served as a reminder of what was now missing from my life.

Maybe, in time, this feeling would go away.

But did I really want that?

I was no longer sure.

CHAPTER TWENTY-SEVEN

Julia

"What are you doing here?" Wes asked when he opened the door and saw me standing on the doorstep. His dark hair was a bit disheveled, his casual attire of a t-shirt and jeans a nice change from the man he was just a few years ago, perpetually clad in a suit, spending nearly every waking hour of his life at the office.

But that was before he met Londyn.

Before he took a risk on her.

Before he realized she was worth any sacrifice.

"I assumed you'd be jet-lagged." My brother held the door open, inviting me inside.

"That's the beauty of flying first class with flatbed seats. You arrive somewhat rested. I did take a little nap today, though. Which is why I'm wide awake now."

I didn't want to tell him I hated being alone in my house with no Imogene to fill the silence with her laughter. Hell, even when she locked herself in her room, earbuds in as she listened to music or FaceTimed with her friends who lived mere houses away, I still found comfort in her presence. With no one there, it brought into sharp focus how alone I truly was. I'd never felt this way before when she wasn't home. At least not like this.

But after spending the week with Lachlan, I seemed to analyze every single aspect of my life with a higher level of scrutiny. Imogene was only a few years away from going to college. Was this how I wanted my future to look? Alone? Scared to take a risk? In the same place I'd always been?

"Well, it's good to see you. To have you back home. Especially after everything." He wrapped me in a tight hug, my five-two frame tiny compared to his over six-foot stature.

"It's really good to be home. To get back to reality."

He pulled back, meeting my gaze. I could see the questions swirling in his eyes. But being the perceptive brother he'd always been, he didn't press me to talk about anything. Not yet anyway.

"You hungry? Londyn made some pork tenderloin for dinner. We have some left if you'd like a plate."

"I'm fine. I could use a glass of wine, though."

"You got it."

I followed him through the foyer and into the open

living space. The instant I entered, Londyn's dark eyes found mine, a smile covering her face.

"You're here." She slowly pulled herself up from the couch, waddling toward me.

I'd only been gone a week, but I swore her stomach had swelled even more. If I didn't know she still had a few months to go, I'd have thought she was ready to give birth any day now.

"How was Hawaii?" she asked as we kissed each other's cheeks. "Judging from the color you got, it looks like it wasn't all work."

I smiled, stealing a glance in my brother's direction, the two of us having an unspoken conversation, much like we did as kids. He didn't have to utter a single syllable for me to pick up on the fact he hadn't told Londyn anything. About Lachlan. About Claire. And especially about Nick.

"I enjoyed myself," I finally said.

It wasn't a lie. I *did* enjoy myself. Probably more than I should have.

"Good." She grabbed my hands, squeezing tightly. "You deserve it, sweetie."

"And how are you?" I asked, pulling my hands from hers. "How are you feeling?"

"Exhausted," she sighed, placing her hand over her stomach. "This one's taking a bit out of me. Speaking of which, I think I'm just going to head up and crawl into bed. It's getting more and more difficult to get comfortable these days. You don't even want to see the pile of pillows I place all around me just to shift position a few minutes later."

I laughed, remembering those days all too well, even though it had been almost fifteen years since I'd given birth.

"It'll all be worth it once that little princess arrives."

"It definitely will." She beamed. "We'll catch up sometime this week, okay? I want to hear all about your trip."

"It's a date."

We hugged again, then she walked over to Wes, giving him a sweet kiss before slowly making her way up the stairs.

Once we were alone, I dropped my voice to no louder than a whisper, just to be on the safe side.

"I assume you haven't told her anything." I arched a brow.

He shook his head, handing me a glass of red wine, then grabbing a glass containing a few fingers of scotch for himself. We made our way over to the couch, assuming our usual positions.

"I don't want to do anything that could cause her stress right now," Wes explained. "At least not until we have more concrete information. Agent Curran is working on getting that, but as I'm sure you can imagine, it could take a while to authenticate every piece of jewelry you received, especially since he needs to get the local authorities involved. He has been able to verify two pieces as belonging to women on Claire's list of potential victims. In the meantime, he hopes you'll allow him access to your employee records. See if maybe there's a connection there."

"Of course. Whatever it takes to get to the bottom of this."

"Great."

I brought my glass to my lips, looking around the room as I took a large sip. When my eyes fell on the enormous television screen, I choked on my wine, coughing, my throat burning from a combination of liquor and surprise.

"You okay?" Wes rubbed my back in a soothing manner as I attempted to get my coughing under control.

It wasn't the fact Wes had his television tuned in to the Atlanta game. Or the fact the man I knew so intimately was currently on the mound. Or even the fact he looked so damn sexy in his uniform.

No. What had me choking on my wine was what I saw sticking out of the back pocket of his perfectly molded pants.

My panties.

That cocky bastard.

"Better?" Wes asked once I finally managed to catch my breath.

I nodded, clearing my throat a few times, trying to not look at the screen. Whenever I did, it brought back memories of the night he stole my panties as a so-called good luck charm.

And the mind-blowing orgasm he gave me with just his fingers.

Then, as luck would have it, the camera zoomed in on his face as he prepared to throw another pitch, intense, blue eyes focused on the catcher's mitt.

It reminded me of the way his stare bore into me while moving inside me, every ounce of attention devoted to making me feel every bit of pleasure possible.

A shiver rolled through me at the memory, my cheeks heating.

"Do you need me to leave you alone? Give you some privacy?" Wes joked.

I quickly snapped out of my daydream and playfully slapped his arm. "Don't be sick."

"Hey. I was just offering. Who knew your kink was younger baseball players?"

My eyes flung wide, shocked to hear him talking like this. He was always the soft-spoken, reserved one. I was the loud one. The one who did everything to pretend she was happy and well-adjusted when nothing could have been further from the truth.

"Younger baseball players are *not* my kink," I protested, albeit lamely.

Okay... Maybe they were.

"And why are we talking about this in the first place?" I continued, flustered. "You're my brother. Plus, *I'm* supposed to be the one being inappropriate. That's my role. I make the jokes while you remain serious and reflective."

"Serious and reflective?"

"Yeah. That's you." I waved my hand down his frame.

"Always studying and analyzing a situation before jumping into a conversation."

"Okay..." His gaze swept over my face, seeming to analyze *me*, which wasn't exactly what I'd intended when I offered my assessment. "So, what happened between you?" He nodded toward the television. "How did you leave things?"

I pushed out a long breath. "On a rain delay with no end in sight."

His forehead wrinkled in confusion. "What do you mean?"

"Exactly what I said. He told me he wanted to be with me. Then told me to not decide anything until I came home and had time to really think about it instead of listening to my gut in the moment."

"And now that you *are* home?"

I sank into the couch, leaning back on the headrest behind me. "I don't fucking know, Wes. One second, I'm all like yes! Amazing sex. Let's do this. Screw the consequences."

"And the next?"

I heaved a sigh, turning my head to meet his gaze. "The next, I'm reminded of what those consequences could be. Of all the reasons this would never work. And trust me, Wes. There are a ton of reasons I shouldn't even be considering this. It's absurd! I'm forty. He's twenty-seven. It's a level of crazy that's so far off the rails, even for me. And I've done some pretty outrageous shit."

"But are they reasons?" he asked calmly, despite my increasingly irritated voice. "Or are they simply excuses?"

"Excuses?" I straightened, setting my wine glass on the coffee table in front of me. "They're not excuses. They're—"

"Listen, Jules," he interrupted, placing his glass beside mine before grabbing my hands in his. "I've been doing a lot of thinking about this, especially after we talked last week. I don't think I've ever heard you as happy as I did the other morning, even after uncovering the possibility someone was emulating Nick's criminal behavior. But that didn't seem to affect you. Instead, I heard something in your voice I didn't think I ever would again."

"What's that?"

"Life."

I exhaled a tiny breath, a small lump forming in my throat. I could deny it all I wanted, but the truth was, my week with Lachlan made me feel more alive than I ever had. Like I was actually living again, instead of simply going through the motions. Simply existing.

"You had a shitty childhood. No one can argue with that. Born to an addict. Sent to foster care. Adopted by a woman as pretty much a pawn for her to appear charitable when she really didn't give two shits about you. Hell, I doubt she gave two shits about me, for that matter, considering she's done nothing to be a part of either of our lives, or her grandkids' lives, since Dad divorced her.

"I didn't notice it back then, probably because

Meemaw and Gampy more than made up for how lacking our parents were. But now that I'm older, now that I have a child of my own with another on the way, I couldn't imagine either of them enduring what you had at the hands of the people entrusted to provide for and love you. Then all that shit with Nick..." He trailed off, jaw tensing in a rare glimpse of anger from my brother, a man who was normally calm and even-tempered, not much truly upsetting him.

"You've spent the majority of your life just trying to survive. I get the feeling that's the only thing you truly know how to do. You make all your choices with that one goal in mind. Now that you've had a taste of something good, something pure, something that comes with no qualifications or requirements, you don't know how to handle it. It's so far from what you're used to that it scares you. Makes you wonder how to protect yourself from this new, frightening scenario called happiness. Wonder how you're going to *survive* this."

"Wes...," I exhaled, unsure what to say.

I never really saw things this way before, but he pretty much hit the nail on the head. Then again, he did have a front-row seat to my lifetime of self-sabotage whenever something good finally happened to me.

It was all I knew.

"Healthy relationships have been the exception for you, not the rule. So when you find yourself in one, or at least on the precipice of the possibility of one, you start to question everything. Start to come up with excuse after excuse about why it'll never work. And do you want to know why?"

"Why?" I choked out, although I had a feeling I already knew the answer.

"The same reason you remained married to Nick for so long. To protect yourself. To protect Imogene. To protect the few people you've allowed into your heart." He tightened his grip on my hands, his expression filled with emotion. "But do you remember what Meemaw used to always say whenever you were having a rough day?"

"What's that?"

"'*Broken crayons—*'"

"'*Still color,*'" I interrupted, remembering my meemaw saying that on more than one occasion, assuring me that even though I may not have lived up to the ridiculous expectations Lydia, my adoptive mother, placed on my shoulders, I was still a source of beauty.

"Exactly. You may see yourself as broken, Jules, but ever since the day my parents brought you home, you've filled my world with color. Maybe it's time to allow someone else to see your color, too, despite your broken pieces.

"All those reasons, all those *excuses* are just that. Excuses. If it's meant to be, you'll find a way to work past all the obstacles. Just look at Londyn and me."

He dropped his hold and leaned back, gaze going to a photo hanging over the mantle of the two of them on their wedding day, their son, Eli, between them.

"Lord knows we had our fair share of obstacles. But not once did we give up on each other. We faced them. Together. It sounds cheesy, but we're stronger together.

"I guess what I'm trying to say is you don't have to go through life alone anymore, Jules. You've got an amazing support system. Me, Londyn, Imogene, and even Dad, now that he's seen what a shitty role model he was when we were younger. We've all got your back. You don't have to keep living in survival mode." He held my gaze for a beat, then a nostalgic gleam covered his expression. "Remember one of Meemaw's other sayings?"

"Which one?" I laughed slightly. "Between Gampy and Meemaw, they could have filled a book with folksy words of wisdom."

"That's certainly true. Thankfully, they passed these pearls of wisdom down to us so we could call on them when we needed them the most. But the one I'm talking about is '*When it feels scary to jump, that's exactly when you jump. Because—*'"

"'*Otherwise, you'll end up staying in the same place your entire life,*'" I finished, my heart warming at the memory of the woman who'd always offered me so much advice. Whose advice I still held dear, even though she'd been gone over twenty years now.

Wes smiled sweetly. "Do you really want to stay in the same place your entire life? Do you really want to stay in *this* place you've been since you met Nick? Or do you finally want to live again?"

I blinked, really taking my brother's words to heart. I looked around his living room, gaze falling on the television once more, watching as Lachlan stepped up to the plate. It brought to mind the night he took me to his little league field in Hawaii. It was my first peek into who Lachlan Hale was underneath the uniform and panty-dropping smile.

He was a *good* person. Would do anything for somebody he loved.

Didn't I deserve to be with someone like him? Maybe Wes was right. Maybe everything else truly didn't matter. That I didn't need to keep making decisions just to survive. Maybe it was time I finally lived again.

I jumped to my feet, my mind racing.

"What is it?" He scrambled up, concerned gaze tracing over me.

"I..." I shook my head, my thoughts a jumbled mess. Except for one. "Do you still have season tickets?"

A sly smile curved his lips. "Right on the first base line. Directly in his line of sight when on the mound."

"I'm going to need one."

CHAPTER TWENTY-EIGHT

Julia

This was absolutely crazy. What the hell was I even thinking, coming out to the stadium in the hopes of Lachlan somehow seeing me in the crowd of tens of thousands of screaming fans. At least I had the good sense to take an Uber instead of driving, then having to park when the game was probably already half over. I just prayed Lachlan was still pitching. Wes said he was usually good for about six or seven innings. I hoped I wasn't too late.

And that he'd miraculously see me.

I followed the overhead signs past different concession stands, dozens of distinct aromas fighting for attention. It reminded me of my childhood. Of all the times Gampy brought Wes and I to this exact stadium to see his beloved team play, even though they were once one of the worst teams in baseball.

Now, according to Wes, they actually had a shot at going all the way this year, thanks to their star pitcher.

Finally finding the section where Wes' season tickets were located, I hurried toward it, showing the usher the ticket on my phone. He nodded, allowing me entry, and I made my way up the ramp.

With every step I took, the sounds grew louder. Fans cheering. A bat cracking as it made contact with the ball. Short, musical interludes when a different batter stepped up to the plate.

When I emerged into the stands, the field coming into view, a rush of excitement filled me. And not the normal rush any lover of baseball experienced at a game. This was different. More personal.

I continued down the concrete steps toward my seat, dozens of fans wearing jerseys with Hale on the back. My choice in clothing, however, didn't remotely resemble appropriate attire for a baseball game, making me feel a bit out of place. I wore a white sundress, for crying out loud.

The same one I wore in Hawaii when Lachlan took me to his ball field.

If that wasn't a sign this was where I was meant to be, I didn't know what was.

As I continued down the stands, my pulse increased, especially as I grew closer and closer to the field. Wes told me his tickets were on the first base line. I didn't expect them to be only two rows behind the dugout.

Atlanta's dugout.

Where I'd have the perfect view of Lachlan as he ran out onto the field or warmed up to bat.

Holy shit. This was really happening.

As I found my seat, a needle of doubt settled, telling me it wasn't too late to back out.

But I was done operating in survival mode. It was time to live again.

I sat, smoothing a hand down my sundress, butterflies flapping in my stomach.

"You a friend of Wes'?"

I glanced behind me at a man I estimated to be in his seventies or eighties. A baseball cap covered his head, and he wore what appeared to be a vintage jersey.

"I'm his sister."

"Julia!" His eyes lit up as he grabbed my hand, shaking it. "It's so nice to finally meet you. Wes has told us all about you." He dropped his hold, then nudged the younger man at his side, whom appeared to be about my age. "This is Wes' sister, Julia. This is my son, Carter."

I smiled at him, extending my hand. "Nice to meet you." Then I looked back at the older man and arched a brow. "And you are?"

"Oh, my apologies. My name's Harold."

"How do you two know Wes?"

He shrugged. "I've had these seats for nearly thirty

years now. And I believe Wes has had his for over ten. Season ticket holders who don't scalp their tickets and actually come to the games become like family. So that's what Wes is now. Family."

"That's nice." I smiled, then started to face forward.

"Carter is single."

I darted my gaze around once more, meeting Harold's devious grin. "Excuse me?"

"Pop," Carter muttered, shaking his head. By his aggravated, yet unsurprised reaction, I got the feeling he dealt with this a lot. "I'm sorry," he said, his voice sincere. "My divorce was recently finalized, and Pop's decided to make it his mission to set me up with every female with a pulse." He glared at his father. "Including my son's nanny."

"She's a very pretty girl," Harold argued in his defense.

"Who's only twenty-three. And my employee. My ex-wife would have a field day with that one." He rolled his eyes.

"Who cares what that woman thinks? She's nothing but a giant pain in the ass."

Harold turned his attention back to me. "So, are you interested in my son? He's got a great job. Makes a lot of money. Has a closet filled with fancy suits. Drives some expensive, electric car. What do you think?"

"I—"

"I'm sure Julia's not superficial enough to care about those things," Carter interjected.

I gave him a smile, then looked back at Harold. "I

appreciate the offer, I suppose. But I'm actually seeing someone."

The words left my mouth before I could really think about them. *Was* I seeing someone? I wasn't sure what Lachlan and I were at the moment. But the ease with which I said it reinforced that this was where I needed to be.

"I hope he knows how lucky he is," Harold said.

"I hope he does, too."

With one more smile, I turned back around, refocusing my attention on the game just as an Atlanta player struck out, bringing the inning to an end.

I squinted at the scoreboard, noting it was going into the top of the fifth. My heart rate kicked up slightly when I saw Lachlan's form appear on the large screens as he made his way out of the dugout.

The dugout that was mere feet in front of me.

I flung my gaze in his direction, my breath catching at how close he was. Regardless, he still seemed like a world away, the wall separating the stands from the field an insurmountable obstacle.

Would he look into the stands? Realize I was here? He seemed so focused on the game. Like it was the only thing that existed. Maybe this was a stupid idea.

But I needed to at least try to get his attention.

Jumping to my feet, I placed my hands around my mouth, praying he'd hear me over the boisterous noise in the stadium.

"Watch out for jellyfish!"

He stopped abruptly, not moving for several long moments, as if he thought he was imagining it.

"Come on," I muttered to myself. "Turn around."

I could sense several pairs of eyes staring at me like I was crazy. Maybe I was.

But this was unlike anything I'd experienced in years.

It made me feel more alive than I had in years.

The butterflies in my stomach steadily increased with every drawn-out second as Lachlan slowly turned and scanned the stands. When his blue eyes landed on me, everything about him shifted. His face lit up, mouth curving in the corners, a weight seeming to lift off his shoulders.

Hi, I mouthed.

He stared, dumbstruck, blinking repeatedly, as if convinced he was imagining this. Then he finally mouthed his reply.

Hi.

He didn't look away, his stare boring into me, stripping me bare, revealing my truth. The reason for my presence here.

I've made my decision. I choose you. More importantly, I choose myself.

Somehow, I sensed he understood all of that without me having to say a word. He treated me to one last smile, then jogged the rest of the way to the mound, glancing my direction after every warmup pitch, as if wanting to make sure I really was here.

I sat back down, exhaling a long breath, small smile on my face.

"So, uh... Lachlan Hale?"

I glanced behind me, meeting Harold's inquisitive look. I could have brushed it off, told him he was just a friend. But if I was going to jump, I was going to fucking jump.

Beaming, I nodded. "Yes. Lachlan Hale."

"Nice catch." He squeezed my shoulder. "Nice catch indeed."

I turned my eyes forward, watching as Lachlan wound up and threw a strike. "I think so, too."

CHAPTER TWENTY-NINE

Lachlan

The sound of my cleats against concrete echoed in the corridor leading from the dugout to the locker room, my feet not carrying me nearly quickly enough.

I never wanted to be taken out of a game as badly as I did tonight. Normally, it was a good night if the pitching staff kept me in for seven innings. Tonight, I stayed in through the eighth. I had a good night. Hell, I had a bloody *great* night, throwing strikes left and right, as if the ball had a direct line straight into my catcher's mitt.

As if I had a good luck charm.

In a way, I did.

I still couldn't believe Julia was here. I almost expected to jolt awake and learn it was all a dream.

But for the first time since I'd said goodbye to her, I was wide awake.

I'd hoped she'd eventually figure out what she wanted and that it would be me. I didn't expect her to figure it out so soon, especially considering she'd only been back in Atlanta for twelve hours.

I guess when you know, you know.

And I knew from the second I felt her skin on mine. It just took my brain a while to catch up to my heart.

Much like Julia.

At least I hoped that was why she was here.

I wasn't going to assume anything yet. I also wasn't going to let her walk out of this ballpark without talking to her.

Which was why I was a man on a mission, jogging through the maze of tunnels, a fluttering sensation in my stomach getting stronger the closer I grew to my destination. And it wasn't the locker room, although I could certainly use a shower after pitching in the Atlanta heat and humidity.

But I didn't want to waste a second.

Julia had already seen me at my absolute worst. Saw my darkness, yet still accepted me.

A little sweat wouldn't faze her.

As I approached one of the security guards stationed outside a room marked "hospitality", he stood, giving me a curt nod, obviously anticipating me.

In between innings, I'd grabbed the equipment

manager and asked him to bring her here. If I hadn't, it would have taken me forever to find her after the game. Sure, I could have jumped on top of the dugout, pulled her into my arms, kissed her right then and there. But I wasn't sure where her head was. And everything I knew about Julia told me this was one conversation we needed to have in private.

Drawing in a deep breath, I did everything I could to steady my nerves. I hadn't been this nervous in a while, even when pitching during the playoffs. That was only a game. And as much as I loved the game, I wanted this more.

Heart thrashing in my chest, I pushed the door open and stepped into the empty room.

Empty except for one person.

At the sound of my footsteps, Julia jumped up from her seat, her eyes immediately darting to mine.

I slowed to a stop mere feet away, chest heaving, stomach fluttering as I took in her appearance.

When I saw her in the stands, I didn't think I'd ever seen anything so beautiful.

My own "Lady in White", like Roy Hobbs had in *The Natural*.

But right now, as her green eyes lit up with a vitality I didn't think possible, she was more than just beautiful.

She was breathtaking. Stunning. Inspiring.

As much as I wanted to wrap her in my arms and lose myself in her, I wouldn't do that. Not until I was certain she wanted this. That she was ready to take a risk.

I'd already faced my fears, allowed myself to be vulnerable, laid myself bare.

It was her turn to do the same. That was the only way I'd know she was truly in this, despite all the challenges we faced.

"Have you made a decision?" I asked softly.

She nodded.

"And?" A twinge of hope filled that one syllable.

She studied me for several moments, chewing on her lower lip, seemingly unsure. Then she pushed out a breath.

"The past few days, I've been on a seesaw of emotions," she declared. "I won't lie to you and tell you this was an easy decision for me. It wasn't. In fact, it's been one of the most difficult things I've ever had to do. Because it made me actually look at who I am. And not just on the outside, but in here." She covered her heart with her hand. "To do that, I had to revisit all the shit I've been through in my life. Let me tell you, that's some pretty heavy baggage."

"Yes, it is," I said evenly. I wouldn't deny her that. It was amazing she was still upright after carrying all the baggage that had weighed her down most of her life.

"But then my brother pointed out something I'd never realized before."

I furrowed my brows. "What's that?"

"He told me I've spent my whole life in survival mode. That every single decision I've ever made has been with one thing in mind..."

"Surviving."

"Yeah." Her lips curved up into a sad smile. "That's all I know how to do, Lachlan. And not out of choice. But because of a lifetime of living on the defensive. So doing anything that has the potential of being risky simply isn't in my DNA. Isn't who I am."

"Oh." My shoulders fell, chest tightening. I wasn't sure I liked where this conversation was headed.

"But I don't want to live like that anymore."

I perked up, hope filling me once more, begging her to give me the answer I'd been desperate to hear ever since I gave her my truth. "You don't?"

She shook her head as she took several slow steps toward me. "I don't. I don't want to just survive anymore. I want to *live*. And when I'm with you..." Tears welled in her eyes. "I've never felt so alive."

She allowed her confession to hang in the air between us for several seconds as I relished in it, unable to find the words to tell her how bloody happy this made me.

"I know we have a lot to work out," she continued when I didn't say anything. "For one, I have to figure out how I'm going to tell my daughter that I'm not only dating a much younger man, but he also plays for her favorite team. Then there's all the stuff with Claire and Nick and Piper and—"

I advanced, clutching her cheeks in my hands, the sudden motion cutting her off. Then I moved my lips against hers, tongue swiping against them in a desperate plea.

When she didn't immediately open for me, I murmured, "Kiss me."

She hesitated for a beat. Then I felt her mouth curve into a smile. I knew exactly what she was remembering. Our first night together.

Our first kiss.

"Is this just a charity kiss?" she teased back, her voice light and playful.

I chuckled, heart expanding with an emotion I couldn't even begin to put into words.

"Like, are you only kissing me because you feel bad?" she continued. "Because if you are—"

"Let me kiss you and you'll see how uncharitable this kiss will actually be. In fact, if I had to describe it, it would be the antithesis of a kiss for charity."

"Is that right?"

"That's right."

I was about to resume the kiss once more when, as expected, Julia pulled back, a smirk on her full, pouty lips.

"And what would one call a kiss that's the antithesis of charity?"

I pinched my mouth into a tight line, feigning deep contemplation. "To come up with the best word, we must first look at the definition of charity."

Dropping my hold, I paced in front of her, imitating my movements of that first night we shared together. "What comes to mind when you hear the word charity?"

"Kindness. Philanthropy..." She paused. "Decency."

Waggling my brows, I stopped pacing, hands returning to her face as I slowly lowered my lips to hers. "Then you should know this kiss will be so indecent, so immoral, so improper, you might consider it offensive."

"Is that right?" she breathed huskily.

"That's right."

"Well then..." She hooked her arm around my neck, seeking out my kiss. "Offend me, you beast."

Growling, I covered her lips with mine, pouring everything we'd been through since that night into this "first" kiss.

And that was what this felt like. Our first kiss all over again. The first kiss after we'd dropped pretenses. Faced our fears. Took a risk.

For years, I guarded my heart, allowed anger to control me.

Until this inexplicable, unexpected, amazing woman managed to weasel her way past every single one of my defenses.

Now, I never wanted to go back to that person I was just a little more than a week ago. Julia said I made her feel alive.

But she taught me how to live again.

And perhaps love again.

I didn't care what this was. Didn't need to label it. All I knew was that this thing we had was real. And I would fight for this, for her, for us, no matter the cost.

Bringing the kiss to an end, I rested my forehead

against hers, peace filling me. I exhaled a tiny breath of air the same time she did.

As I drew in her breath, drinking her in, I felt the connection between us strengthen even more.

"I don't care what obstacles we may face in the future, Julia," I began, cupping her cheeks. "We'll get through them. Together."

She covered my hands with hers, basking in my reassurance. "Together."

"Yes." I pressed my lips to hers once more. "Together."

CHAPTER THIRTY

Nick

Chains rattled against concrete in the long empty corridor as Domenic Jaskulski shuffled the best he could with the shackles around his ankles, two guards in front, two behind.

Nick could just barely make out the occasional, faint *buzz* of doors being opened and closed, but otherwise, it was relatively quiet in this area of the prison.

Or as quiet as anywhere in a prison could possibly be.

"You know the drill," one of the obtuse guards grunted in an unrefined, Southern accent that gave all people from this part of the country the reputation of being an inbred hillbilly.

Nick had zero patience for those who had no desire to

better themselves. To educate themselves. It made him wild with rage.

But he wouldn't act on it.

It was important he not draw any attention to himself.

Otherwise, the plan to finally be reunited with his one true love would fall apart.

He couldn't have that.

"Would you be so kind as to remind me of the *drill* again, Officer?" Nick asked, his voice exuding superiority and class. "I don't believe I quite remember, as I've only been doing this *very* thing every week for the past several years."

"Enough with the snotty remarks, jackass."

The officer opened the door, practically pushing Nick into the room, causing him to stumble slightly. Grabbing his elbow, he dragged him toward the table where a man dressed in black sat, patiently waiting for their weekly spiritual advisement.

"But I do so enjoy our banter. I find our conversations quite...invigorating. Intellectually stimulating. Why, just last week, I was surprised to learn you knew the proper use of regardless, instead of using *irregardless*. I'll be honest. Hearing some of your brethren utter that abomination makes me just...murderous."

"Shut it, asswipe," the officer ordered, all but shoving him onto the cold, metal chair. "Or I'll revoke your visitation privileges for the next month, *irregardless* of whether it's a clergy visit."

The officer retrieved a key from his belt, forcing Nick's hands on the table. With rough motions, he secured the cuffs to the bar in the center, shot Nick a glare, then retreated from the stark, cold room.

Unlike the other visitation rooms, there were no windows. No cameras. Nothing.

There couldn't be. It wasn't allowed when inmates met with their lawyers or spiritual advisors. It was truly the only place one could conduct any conversation in private.

And, for these conversations, privacy was essential.

Once the heavy door slammed shut, the *buzz* indicating it was locked, Nick slowly lifted his eyes to the young man sitting across the table, a leather-bound bible in front of him.

He pushed it toward Nick, who opened it to a book in *The Old Testament. Leviticus*, to be precise. When his eyes fell on a photo, his heart skipped a beat, a slow smile curving on his lips at the woman in the image.

Beautiful.

Naked.

Dead.

"Forgive me, Father," Nick began, slowly raising his gaze to meet a pair of clear, blue eyes, "for I believe *you* have sinned."

The visitor's lips twisted up in the corners, his devious grin nearly identical to Nick's.

"You know what they say. Like father, like son."

I hope you enjoyed Persuasion! Julia and Lachlan's story continues in Provocation! Will Julia and Lachlan's relationship survive in the real world, especially when more information comes to light indicating danger is closer than they thought? Find out today! Scan the code to the right or enter the below web address into your browser to grab your copy!

https://www.tkleighauthor.com/temptationseries

* * *

I appreciate your help in spreading the word about my books. Please leave a review on your favorite book site.

PROVOCATION

One week. No names. No expectations.

That was our agreement.

We were supposed to walk away once our time in Hawaii was over.

No matter what.

But that was before I finally decided to take a risk and jump.

And that's precisely what being involved with Lachlan Hale is... A risk.

Between the complications that go along with dating a

celebrity and the real possibility that my ex-husband is still watching my every move, there are times I question whether it's worth it.

Whether I'm selfishly putting Lachlan's life at risk, too.

But like he promised... We'll get through it. Together.

Until the bottom drops in a way I never could have anticipated.

Lines are drawn.
Loyalties are tested.
And I'm stuck in the middle, engaged in a fierce battle between my head and my heart.

And there can only be one winner.

https://www.tkleighauthor.com/temptationseries

PLAYLIST

Joke's on You - Charlotte Lawrence
I'm Not Ok - The Sweeplings
Surrender - Birdy
There's No Way - Lauv & Julia Michaels
Bitter Tonic - Kings Elliot
Sanctuary - Weshly Arms
I've Seen You Naked - Such Stefano
This is How You Fall in Love - Jeremy Zucker, Chelsea Cutler
Tell Me - Hunter Hayes
Don't - Jade Jones
Dance With Me - Phillip Phillips
Biblical - Callum Scott
Don't Let Me Go - Cigarettes After Sex
First Light - Spencer Jones

Be My Mistake - The 1975
At My Worst - Pink Sweat$
Found - Jacob Banks
Unholy War - Jacob Banks

ACKNOWLEDGMENTS

Woo hoo! Book two is done! We're halfway there. (And now *Livin' on a Prayer* is stuck in your head. LOL.)

I have to admit. I am having a blast with this story. For those of you who just recently started following me and have only known me to write angsty contemporary romance, that's not where I got my start.

My first several books were actually romantic suspense, which is probably what most people tend to know me for. While I've taken a break from it the past few years to work on something lighter and less...murdery, I'm so thrilled to be back to my roots.

Writing any book, whether it be a straightforward contemporary romance or a more suspenseful story with tons of twists and turns, is a labor of love. And I wouldn't be able to do it without the amazing team I have supporting me.

First and foremost, a huge thanks to my husband, Stan, and daughter, Harper Leigh. I couldn't do this without their support.

To my wonderful PA and alpha reader, Melissa Crump — Thank you so much for everything you do to keep me on task. And for not calling me crazy when I message you saying I'm changing something... Like covers for a completely different series when I'm on a deadline with this one. LOL. You're the best, babe!

To my fantastic beta readers — Lin, Sylvia, Stacy, and Vicky — thanks for reading and offering your feedback on this story. Can't wait to share book three with you!

To my amazing editor — Kim Young. You are a godsend. I'd be lost without you. Thank you so much for working on my babies.

To my girl, A.D. Justice. You complete me. That is all.

To my admin team - Melissa, Vicky, Lea, Joelle. Thanks for keeping my reader group and Facebook page running. Love you ladies!

To my review team. Thanks for always taking the time to read and review my work, even if I make you suffer through some cliffhangers. Don't lie. You love them... LOL.

To my reader group. Thanks for being my super-fans and giving me a place to go when I need a break from writing.

And last but not least, a big thank you to YOU! My amazing readers. Whether this is your first T.K. book or you've read all of them, I'm so grateful you took a chance on my stories.

Stay tuned for the continuation of Lachlan & Julia's story! Will their love survive in the real world? Find out soon!

Love & Peace,

~ T.K.

ABOUT THE AUTHOR

T.K. Leigh is a *USA Today* Bestselling author of romance ranging from fun and flirty to sexy and suspenseful.

Originally from New England, she now resides just outside of Raleigh with her husband, beautiful daughter, rescued special needs dog, and three cats. When she's not writing, she can be found training for her next marathon or chasing her daughter around the house.

facebook.com/tkleighauthor

instagram.com/tkleigh

tiktok.com/@tkleigh

bookbub.com/authors/t-k-leigh

pinterest.com/tkleighauthor

www.ingramcontent.com/pod-product-compliance
Lightning Source LLC
Chambersburg PA
CBHW010841190726
48286CB00012BA/2940